The Mystery on the
by June

The Mystery on the Miniature Railway

CHAPTER ONE
The Journey Begins

WHEN Professor Mark Hills boarded the rear carriage of the 12.30 miniature railway from Heath to Downsend that fateful Friday morning in late September, he thought it would be a practical and enjoyable way to survey the terrain. The eminent nuclear scientist was on his way to a top-secret meeting with other scientists to discuss the future of Downsend Nuclear Power Station, which was being de-commissioned. Professor Hills was hoping to persuade his colleagues, and a couple of government ministers, that vast areas of Romsey Marsh could become an underground bunker built to store the country's nuclear waste.

The Professor had spent the last twenty years working on a system to re-process toxic nuclear waste and transform it into electricity, using all the nuclear elements and leaving what little remained as harmless by-product. The machinery he had invented to perform this process he called the Nuclear Waste Reprocessing System (NWRS), which would finally be unveiled to his colleagues at Downsend. He was also looking forward to meeting up with Ray, a.k.a. Dr Raymond Wells, Head of Downsend C, who was a friend from University. He fondly remembered their times together discussing the latest trends in physics and arguing for one theory against another. Those were exciting times for nuclear scientists, with new theories about particles coming out almost monthly. The Professor had decided there and then to devote the rest of his life into exploring new ways of using nuclear for the good of mankind, whereas his friend had taken a more practical route. Nonetheless, they had seen each other through good times and bad – their marriages, the

1

birth of children, and his subsequent divorce from Alison, his childhood sweetheart.

The little train trundled along the track at quite a pace, blowing its horn whenever it approached a level crossing or a station. At Heath the route took them past the rear of people's gardens, with some people waving as they went. Then it reached into the countryside, where the lambs and horses seemed used to seeing and hearing the little train, taking scant notice. The weather was windy but dry, allowing a good view of his surroundings. Mentally he began ticking off boxes: flat terrain, good for juggernauts; remote location, in case of accidents. The Professor knew all about accidents, for he'd had a few over the years while dealing with nuclear material. This had left him with a type of brittle asthma which could occur suddenly without any warning. His friend had known of this and advised him to sit in the rear carriage of the train, as far away from the smoke as possible. All his experimentation would be worth it, he thought, if he could help make the world a safer place.

The Professor had been very secretive about his work and kept each process separately on a series of ten memory sticks, which he had hidden in various locations. These were only used on a computer which had no internet connection. For his meeting today he had printed out a diagram from each memory stick and collated them into a presentation, which was kept inside his locked, monogrammed briefcase, clutched tightly on his lap.

Loud shrieking from the whistle brought him back from his daydreaming, as the train slowed to a halt. Looking through his window the Professor could see several sheep running down the track, being chased by a tall man with a shepherd's crook. This man then strode along the side of the train, heading in his direction. When he had nearly reached the end of the train, two men seated in the carriage in front of him got out and stood either side of his compartment. One of them politely asked, "Can you get out, please?"

Puzzled, he was about to comply but then suddenly felt threatened and clasped his briefcase even more tightly. The tall man then slid the door on his left hand side open and reached inside with the shepherd's crook, pulling him out. The other two men grabbed him and stopped him running away. The Professor struggled and shouted, his voice disappearing under the noise of the train's whistle. Just as the train gave a particularly long blow on its horn, the large man punched him squarely on the forehead, and everything went white.

CHAPTER TWO
Sounding the Alarm

WHEN the miniature steam locomotive, *Green Dawn*, arrived late at Downsend terminal with an empty rear carriage and no sign of Professor Hills, his reception party were most concerned. Dr Wells, the chief scientist at Downsend C, questioned the driver as to whether there had been any problems en-route. Len, a volunteer driver at the RHLR railway since the 1980s, confirmed that there had been a ten minute delay between St Joseph's Bay and Romsey Warren when some sheep were spotted on the track, and he'd had to wait for the farmer to retrieve them. Apart from that, nothing untoward had occurred. Dr Wells tried calling the Professor's mobile on several occasions with no success. It was at this point that he called the Police.

The local constabulary made a few enquiries, starting at Heath Station. The Guard confirmed that a tall man in a suit and red tie had boarded the rear carriage of the train, which had otherwise been empty at the time. Being the last week of September and out of season, he had only sold ten tickets for the whole trip. The train stopped at every station, and the Driver recalled that the family who were sitting behind him for the entire ride had disembarked at New Romsey to visit the railway museum and then re-joined it in time for the onward journey, but that no-one else had boarded or left the train en-route. The local police then escalated their concerns to DCI Simon Willis, head of Romsey Police.

DCI Willis spoke with Dr Wells and soon realised that if Professor Hills had been kidnapped, as it appeared, this could have national security implications. He then escalated the incident to MI8 Military Intelligence, who asked to be kept informed on an hourly basis. Meanwhile, DCI Willis ordered his officers to search the area around all the station stops, being Heath, Little Church, St Joseph's Bay, New Romsey, Romsey Sands and Downsend in case the good professor had simply got confused and disembarked at the wrong stop. Indeed, it was not unknown for people with very stressful jobs to have nervous breakdowns and he could be wandering around suffering from complete amnesia or worse, suicidal.

Romsey Police, meanwhile, had managed to find seven of the ten passengers who were on board the train from Heath, who were questioned about whether they had seen or heard anything unusual. There had been twelve carriages on the train. The first four passengers were a family with two young sons who had boarded carriage number one directly behind the driver, as their boys had wanted to get as close as possible to the engine. They could not recall seeing any of the other passengers.

The passengers in carriage five had consisted of an elderly couple and a female relative. Mr and Mrs Gower and her sister all remembered seeing Professor Hills getting into the last carriage. Her sister, Irene, who had been sitting facing the rear, did recall two middle-aged men boarding the second to last carriage just before the train set off. They all recounted seeing a farmer waving his stick at the sheep before getting the animals off the track, and Irene had been so amused by the incident that she had changed her seat to watch the proceedings. All interviewed said that the driver had sounded his horn very loudly for several minutes in order to frighten the sheep away, and they had been so interested in the incident that they had not noticed anything else.

There was nothing unusual by itself in two middle-aged men travelling on the light railway. The RHLR had countless admirers, many consisting of middle-aged males. Indeed, the railway would find it difficult to survive without them. But, as these men were the only passengers not to come forward after a public appeal for witnesses, they had to be considered prime suspects in the disappearance of Professor Hills.

Various other scenarios were also debated, including whether the Professor had simply taken the opportunity to disappear himself. Detectives were sent to his home address and his ex-wife and adult children were questioned, as well as computers confiscated.

DCI Simon Willis, in charge of local investigations, requested the London Metropolitan Police be drafted in to assist. The latter then despatched all their spare dog handling units to the scene and were currently scouring the Romsey countryside, much to the consternation of local farmers worried about their stock. The public had also been asked to search their sheds and outbuildings for any sign of Professor Hills, or to report anything unusual occurring in the area.

The first breakthrough in confirming that something untoward had happened was when Farmer Collins, the owner of the escaped sheep, denied appearing on the track waving a stick. He said that he had received a phone call to say that some sheep had escaped, but by the time he arrived they were back in the field. He had then noticed that the wire on his fence had been cut. There also appeared to be signs of a struggle in a field nearby, and a scrap of red material was found on some barbed wire on the fence. This being autumn and the fields very muddy, it was easy to follow three sets of footprints across the field leading to a cycle path running parallel to the railway. On first inspection the imprints appeared quite deep, possibly indicating that the persons had been carrying a heavy load. The cycle path then adjoined a local dirt track, where tyre prints from a vehicle led to a local road and then disappeared.

DCI Willis immediately updated MI8 on these developments. They requested that the scrap of material be checked for DNA evidence to confirm that this had, indeed, been worn by Professor Hills, and that the rear and second-last carriages be kept at New Romsey depot and taped off until forensics arrived. The professor was now classed as officially missing, presumed kidnapped. At five o'clock, after no sightings or contact from Professor Hills, the event was escalated to a 'Category A' and the Prime Minister was informed. An all ports alert was put into place and a meeting of the COBRA committee convened for Saturday morning.

MI8 then despatched two Chinook helicopters from Vauxhall to Downsend carrying a team of 100 specialist investigators. A temporary HQ was set up at Downsend C to collate all the data as it was gathered.

CHAPTER THREE
COBRA Alert

THE PRIME MINISTER headed an emergency meeting of the COBRA Committee, the government's secretive twelve-man circle responsible for national security. This included the heads of the Armed Forces, MI8 secret service, and other select invitees.

"Yesterday our most eminent Nuclear Scientist was apparently kidnapped from a miniature railway in Romsey, en-route to a meeting with the processing team at Downsend. The purpose of that meeting was top-secret and not disclosed to anyone outside of the team, apart from members of the Cabinet and Defence inner circles."

There was a murmur of horror from his colleagues. The PM held his hand up to silence them, then nodded to his personal secretary to start a slide presentation. A photo of a middle-aged man with greying hair and glasses appeared on the screen with the heading 'Professor Mark Hills'.

"You will know that we are looking for a site to store the country's nuclear waste, with Downsend C being a likely candidate. We had issued a press release to explain about the nuclear bunker idea. What we didn't tell them, and indeed is top secret and not allowed to be divulged, was that Professor Hills was taking plans for a new prototype machine to the plant. He has invented a method with the ability to process nuclear waste and turn it into harmless electricity, thus resolving the problem of what to do with the waste and, at the same time, adding significantly to the electrical supply of the nation via the national grid."

A murmur of excitement went round the room.

"The man's a genius!" exclaimed Rear Admiral Hansey.

"Quite," agreed the PM. "I don't need to spell out how important this could be for the nation. But now that he has disappeared, it is our top priority to find out what happened to him and indeed, whether he is still alive."

"Who else knew about this method?" queried a member of the Cabinet.

"Only half a dozen people, and Professor Hills. They were myself, the Deputy PM, Head of MI8 and two colleagues of Professor Hills. This discovery is so secret that we are not able to patent it as yet, for obvious reasons."

The secretary forwarded the presentation and an image of Dr Wells appeared on the screen. The PM spoke to him.

"Good morning, Dr Wells, thank you for joining us. Can you hear us clearly?"

"Good morning, Prime Minister and gentlemen. Yes, I can see and hear you all loud and clear.

"Good, well that's a relief. Can you please explain what plans you had for Professor Hills' visit, starting with yesterday?"

"Yes, certainly. He was due to arrive at 12.05 at Downsend Station, and I and two colleagues were waiting to drive him to the power station entrance, which is still some distance from there."

"I see. And can I ask, why was he travelling on the light railway?"

"He actually asked to. Apart from the novelty factor, he wanted to survey the surroundings to see whether the area was suitable for his plans."

"Understood. Well, that sounds feasible. And what did you have planned for him for the rest of the day?"

"We were going to take him to lunch and then on an escorted tour of the facility. Friday afternoon was going to be an introduction to the processing team, then he was due to give us a presentation at 3.30. He was going to stay in a hotel in New Romsey for the weekend, before starting trials this coming week."

"Thank you, Dr Wells. So who else would have known about this visit?"

"Myself and my two colleagues, and they only knew about it the day before. The rest of the staff were informed that we were going to have a safety audit in the afternoon, in order that they would tidy the place up. They weren't told who Professor Hills really was, or about the testing next week."

"Good, so that narrows things down from a security point of view. What about the hotel, what did you say to them?"

"He was booked in under the name of 'Mr Hills', so I shouldn't have thought they would have spotted anything unusual."

"May I ask a question?" The Head of the Army raised his hand.

"Yes, go ahead," nodded the PM.

"I wondered why the Professor chose to sit in the rear carriage? Only, that has made things much easier for the kidnappers, if that is indeed what has happened to him."

"Did you hear that, Dr Wells? Do you know why he sat in the rear carriage?"

Dr Wells coughed and looked embarrassed.

"Actually, that was my suggestion. The Professor suffers quite badly from asthma, so I advised him to sit as far away from the engine smoke as possible."

"Oh yes, I see. Well, that's one of those unfortunate coincidences, but it has made things easier for the kidnappers, as my colleague said. Now I'd like to hand over to Peter Mason, Head of Intelligence at MI8, to give his views on the situation."

A smartly dressed older man marched to the front of the room.

"Prime Minister, Dr Wells, gentlemen, what we have here is a very serious situation and we need to consider our

10

next actions very carefully. Obviously, suspicion must fall on foreign governments as the most likely candidates. The only question is, who? We must be careful not to offend our Allies in this respect; for example, the Americans."

"Remember *Concorde*?" the Rear Admiral spoke up again. "I don't think we can rule them out completely."

A murmur went round the room, and Peter Mason put his hand up to silence them.

"Everyone, no doubt, will have their personal opinion on who has done this. But we cannot act on speculation in such a delicate matter, we have to look at the facts. I think the key candidates here would be the Chinese and the Russians, but these days one couldn't rule out an Islamic or Israeli connection. Having looked at the precision in the way this kidnap was carried out, my first thought would be the Russians."

Nods of agreement went round the room.

"I would suggest that the only way to ensure that Professor Hills does not leave the country is by involving the military in roadblocks, and a complete ban on flights from Lydd Airport. I would also suggest Navy patrols around the Romsey coast, and extra checks on all sailings from Dover and trains in the Eurotunnel. In effect, a lock-down on all movements in and out of the country, as far as possible."

"Are the police coordinating their searches with the military and MI8?" the PM asked.

"Yes. It's obviously too much to expect Romsey Police to search and make enquiries over such a large and remote area as Romsey Marsh by themselves, so as of 1800 hours yesterday the Metropolitan Police joined forces, principally using their dog handlers. There are a lot of farms and outbuildings in the area, not to mention caravan sites and holiday camps, which is going to make searching extremely difficult. Difficult, but not impossible. My team have set up an HQ at Downsend under my deputy, Craig Bennett. As the military are involved, they will also report to him. The police enquiries are headed up by DCI Willis."

"Is he also based at Downsend?" asked the PM.

"Not as yet, sir."

"I think it would be a good idea, to assist communication between the teams."

"I will get onto it straight away. One of the things he has asked me is, how much information should the Police leak to the public? They have already put out a request for information in the local area, because we are going to need the public's assistance. This was picked up in last night's national news."

"Yes, I did see that. It's a delicate balancing act. The locals will obviously be aware that something major has happened because we are going to saturate the area with police and military personnel. But, and I must stress this, we cannot tell them about the top secret plans for the nuclear reprocessing plant, or the fact that the Professor was carrying this information. Now, is that clear, everyone?"

"Can we inform the DCI?" asked the Army chief.

"No." Peter Mason paused. "What we are going to tell him is that there has been a breach of security at the plant, which may or may not involve the Professor. Is everyone clear on that?"

The room all spoke in agreement.

"Thank you gentlemen, Dr Wells. If you have any queries please contact Mr Mason or myself. Now as speed is of the essence here, I will not detain you any longer."

The PM's Secretary turned off the presentation, and the doors to the meeting room at No. 10 were opened for the attendees to depart.

CHAPTER FOUR
Over to HQ

PETER MASON disembarked from the Chinook helicopter in the grounds of Downsend Power Station where he was met by Dr Wells and the two other members of his team. He had been thrilled by the journey, his first on a Chinook, but also daunted when he saw the vast expanse of Romsey Marsh unfold beneath him.

"Good afternoon, Mr Mason." Dr Wells shook his hand warmly.

"Good afternoon, pleased to meet you," he shouted back. "Shall we get away from these noisy machines before we start a conversation?"

"Yes, good idea." Dr Wells ushered his colleagues and Peter Mason's team towards the enormous structure of the power station that dominated the landscape.

"It's quite an impressive sight," Mason remarked as they reached the main entrance.

"And we've been fascinated by the helicopters," Dr Wells replied, indicating towards the windows, which were full of workers peering through them. "Your colleague, Mr Bennett, has started work on the HQ office.

The Doctor steered them past the Visitor Centre and through to a large rectangular room on the ground floor. They were followed in by the hundred other personnel who had jumped out of the helicopters. These men, and a handful of women, had been handpicked by Peter Mason himself, and included experts in foreign languages and hostage situations.

The room had been hastily set up in classroom style with a projector at the front and rows of tables and chairs borrowed from the staff canteen, each table holding two computers. The room had been divided into four sections:

ID / Transport / Communications / Logistics. IT engineers were busy linking these to an encrypted server dedicated to HQ use only. Mason could see his Deputy deep in discussions with them, and decided to leave him to it.

"This looks eminently suitable, Dr Wells. Well done on setting this up at such short notice."

"Thank you!" He relished the praise for all their hard work. "Though I'm not quite sure where the police and the military are going to stay," he admitted.

"Don't worry about the military, I believe they are setting up camp outside."

"Oh! What about the facilities?"

Peter Mason smiled. This incident was the biggest threat to national security at present and all the Doctor could worry about were the toilet arrangements.

"Don't worry, they will take care of all that themselves."

"Right." The Doctor looked relieved.

"Now I wanted to ask you a few questions about Professor Hills, if I may? Firstly, how well did you know him?"

"Mark and I go back a long way, to Cambridge University in the 70s. I met him there at one of the lectures, although we were on different courses. He was more interested in experimental physics and I studied particle physics."

"I see. Not that I pretend to know much about physics, of course," Mason admitted, "but were you aware of the Professor's plans for, as I understand it, a new processing machine?"

"No. Mark was always very secretive about his ideas. I did have a very broad understanding of the theory, but I believe he was holding back on at least one component of the mechanism, because I could not work out how he was going to do it."

"And did you see any diagrams or papers that he had written?"

"No, that's just it. He was bringing them to show us when he was abducted. That's why we're so worried about him. He's really quite asthmatic and any stress could bring on an attack."

Mason felt a pang of regret that he had not given the Professor's well-being that much thought. He had been more interested in the security implications and the Professor's missing diagrams. That was what this job did to you, he thought ruefully; turned you into an unfeeling machine.

"Yes, of course, it must be very worrying. So he never sent you any details on the internet?"

"I'm afraid not. He was concerned about his ideas being intercepted."

"Mm, very wise. But now, unfortunately, it seems that somebody has intercepted him."

Dr Wells shook his head. "It does look that way. Because I'm sure that Mark would not have done this deliberately. He was absolutely dedicated to his work, and to the future of nuclear in this country."

One of Mason's aides ran up to him. "Excuse me sir, sorry to interrupt, but the head of US Secret Service has asked for an urgent telephone update."

"Right. Excuse me, Doctor." Mason sighed. This was going to be awkward. He didn't want to give too much away and he also wanted to find out how much the Americans knew about the Professor's work.

Meanwhile, he had mentally filed the information supplied by Dr Wells:

1. He had arranged the Professor's meeting and knew where he would be sitting on the train.

2. He knew the Professor was asthmatic and that any stress could be life-threatening.

3. They knew each other at University, and had studied in similar fields.

4. The Professor had been about to reveal a new invention which could revolutionise the nuclear industry.

One could never rule out the possibility of professional rivalry and long-held grudges, he thought to himself, as he walked to a private spot to make his telephone call.

After twenty minutes Mason's ears were red hot, both from his mobile phone and from what the Director of USSS had said to him. He had to assure him that yes, they would check the ports, the Channel Tunnel and the airports and no, they did not need any help from the US military in the search. He could just imagine them crawling all over Downsend nuclear facility and upsetting just about everybody.

Mason headed back to Dr Wells, who showed him into a compact side room which in reality was a cleared out stationery cupboard containing a small desk and computer.

"Will this room be big enough for you, Peter?" asked the Doctor nervously.

"Yes, this is fine. I'm not planning to be here every day, that will be Craig's job. Mine is to run HQ in London, because there are other things going on besides this incident that I need to keep an eye on."

"Oh dear, nothing too serious, I hope?"

"Potentially, Dr Wells, but nothing for you to worry about. This office will be perfect for me. Now if you will excuse me, Doctor, our Allies have demanded a few answers to some questions and I need to get my facts straight."

"Of course. And please, call me Ray."

"Thank you, Ray. If I need to ask you about anything, I'm sure I'll be speaking to you again."

"Yes, anything at all. If it helps to find Mark, I'll be only too happy to assist."

"Thank you, much appreciated."

Dr Wells left Mason to his task as he called out to a young man walking past.

"Can I speak to you a minute? Malcolm, can you update me on the Ferry situation, please?"

"Yes Sir, it takes two and a half hours from Dover to Calais. We believe the Professor went missing at around 12.45 on Friday. The first sailing that he could have made would have been the 13.55, arriving in Calais at 15.35 French time. We've had the ports on alert since 5 o'clock on Friday and the French police have been checking arrivals since then. We've also seconded a dozen British police to assist them."

"Good, so that route is covered now, we hope. What about the Chunnel?" He called it by its original nickname.

"The Eurotunnel? Again, the first train he could have been on was the 2 o'clock from Folkestone, which takes 35 minutes to arrive in Calais. Now, we did alert them at 5pm to search all outward bound vehicles, especially vans and lorries, but we were too late to cover the 2pm departure. We did notify the French authorities, however."

"Hmm, that could be a weak point. So theoretically, he could have already left the country?"

Malcolm looked embarrassed. "Yes sir. But again, we now have British policemen checking arrivals."

"And what about patrolling the coastline?"

"We've got a Navy frigate and some patrol vessels scouring the coast. We had to rely on the Smallstone lifeboat station to begin with."

"Excellent! Good lateral thinking."

"Thank you, sir.

"Okay. I just need to be kept updated so that I can report to the PM's office on an hourly basis. I'd appreciate any news on how the search is going so I'll have something to tell him."

"Yes, will do."

17

"Thanks. Okay, I'll let you get on. William!"

Another young man rushed to Mason's side. "What's the latest on the Airports?"

"Lydd Airport is on lock-down, but nothing has flown from there since yesterday, anyway."

"Well that's a huge relief. What measures are they taking at Gatwick and Heathrow?"

"Since 5pm on Friday they've been doing extra baggage handling checks, not just on x-ray but actually opening up the hand luggage."

"I bet we're extremely popular at the minute."

"And there's no last-minute bookings allowed, it's been changed to 24 hours' notice at the earliest."

"Great idea! Well, sounds as if we're doing our best on that front. Although with millions of passengers flying every day, it's never going to be perfect."

"No, sir."

"Keep me updated regularly on everything, won't you?"

"Yes, will do."

"And if you find Tom G, can you send him my way?"

"Yes, sir."

"Oh look, there he is, can you send him over to me?"

William rushed off to retrieve him.

"Hello Tom, how are the roadblocks going?"

"No sign of the Professor, sir, but some interesting discoveries."

"Such as?"

"Five illegal immigrants in the back of a lorry, several drugs-related finds, and a child who was being abducted by her estranged Egyptian father."

"Well, excellent news! One less heartache for her mother, even if the Professor is no-where to be found."

"Yes, sir."

"And what about the railways?"

"We've got police and sniffer dogs at Ashlea and Ebbsfleet International, and the Professor's description has been circulated to all stations and terminals."

"Excellent. His photo's been shown on the national news, because I've seen it. We've just got to hope for a lucky break now. Thanks, Tom. Just keep me updated regularly, won't you?"

"Will do, sir."

Mason walked over to his deputy. "Everything going to plan, Craig?"

The young man looked flustered. "We're trying to set up a satellite link to GCHQ so that we can put a trace on the professor's mobile phone."

"I thought it looked complicated. Don't let me stop you, I want to have a look at my office before we speak to the team."

"Okay, sir, whenever you're ready."

Mason retired to his office, which in reality was claustrophobic, with no natural light. He didn't plan to spend much time in there unless absolutely necessary. He wandered over to the kitchen area, borrowed a mug from one of the cupboards and made himself a coffee.

The revelation of the rescued child had affected him deeply, although he had shown no sign of it. Fifteen years ago his daughter, Rebecca, had been abducted – physically and mentally, by her mother he thought to himself, and sighed. Their marriage had broken up just as he had been promoted to Head of External Affairs when Karen, his wife, had accused him of being cold and uncaring towards her and sued for divorce. Maybe she had a point, he thought sadly. He had then not seen his three year old daughter for 18 months after Karen had fled to her parents in Australia. When she deigned to return, little Becky had become nervous of her father and cried when he came to take her out for the day. Mason should have tried harder, he knew that, but it had ripped him apart just as if a sharp knife had been thrust into his stomach. The memories were as vivid as yesterday. He sat quietly in his box room for ten minutes and drank the coffee quietly before wandering back to HQ.

The IT guys flown over in the Chinook had wired up a microphone and laptop to the front desk, and Mason thought it time to speak to his staff.

"Okay everybody, may I have your attention?" The room fell silent. "It seems like everyone has pretty much grabbed a table and chair and a computer for themselves, is that right?"

A hundred yes, sirs rang out.

"Good. Has Craig given everyone a list of their responsibilities?"

Some dissent went round the room. Craig stepped forward.

"Everybody has been assigned to either Team A or Team B. Team A will be working all night until 8am, and then Team B will be here – ON TIME – tomorrow morning to take over their twelve hour shift. Does everyone know whether they are on Team A or B?"

"Yes," came the reply.

"Good. Does everyone know who their counterpart is in Team A or Team B?"

A few no's sounded.

"Well, it is your duty to find that out before you leave here this evening – those of you who are leaving. How many people don't know, raise your hands?"

Ten people raised their right arm.

"That's a nice even number. I would suggest that the ten of you get together over here and find out who is buddying who, because the chances are your missing partner is in this group."

The ten made their way sheepishly to the front.

"You need to know your other half, so to speak, because you will be hot-desking, so please be considerate and clear your desk each day before you change over. We've booked you all into the Holiday Hotel in Ashlea, which is still quite a drive but about the nearest hotel we could find. So there will be one coach transferring Group A to the hotel at 0800 hours tomorrow morning, whilst another coach will be collecting Group B from the hotel at 7.30am sharp and bringing them here. Is that clear, everyone?"

"Yes, sir," came back the response.

"Is there anything you wish to add?" Craig asked his boss. Mason stepped up to the mic.

"Yes, I'd like to remind you all that secrecy is of the utmost importance. So remember in the hotel not to talk about what you have seen or heard in HQ, is that clear?"

"Yes, sir," came the response again.

"Okay, well I shall be flying back to London tonight and leaving you in Craig's capable hands, but if you need to reach me you all have my priority phone number. Dr Wells has kindly arranged for the staff canteen to remain open until 6 o'clock, so I suggest you go there and stock up on food and drink for the evening. And remember to keep your receipts. All right, that's it for now."

Craig quickly took back the mic.

"Those of you leaving this evening, please be ready in Reception at 6.30. That's all."

A sudden din of excited voices filled the air as the agents raced off to the canteen.

"All right, I'm heading back home now, Craig, but can you keep me updated every couple of hours, until 10pm at least?"

"Yes, I will."

"And let me know straight away if anything significant comes up, for example if you manage to trace the Professor's telephone."

"Certainly, sir."

"Oh, and another thing." Mason moved to within earshot. "Can you put a trace on Dr Wells' mobile and home telephone number too?"

He registered the shock on Craig's face.

"Oh, right. Will do."

Mason smiled to himself. Craig was very good, granted, but he still had a lot to learn. As for him, he was going to turn up unannounced at his daughter's flat tonight and see whether she would let him in. He felt a desperate need to see her again.

CHAPTER FIVE
Willis takes stock

DCI WILLIS called together his team at Sussex Police HQ in Middlestone. Twenty officers crammed into one of the small meeting rooms on his floor.

"Thank you, ladies and gentlemen."

The room fell quiet.

"I've just been speaking with my counterpart at MI8 regarding the kidnapping incident at Downsend. There's still no sign of Professor Hills and in view of the national security implications we are going to set up a joint task force to investigate the incident. Now, I've just heard that the Prime Minister has requested that we all decamp to Downsend Power Station for the course of the investigation so that we can coordinate our work with the security forces, the military and Romsey Police. If there's anyone here who would be unable to do so, please come and see me after this meeting."

A murmur went round the floor.

"I shouldn't need to tell you that this work is of an extremely sensitive nature, so I don't want any discussions about it outside of the team. At the moment we are treating the Professor's disappearance as unexplained but reading between the lines, there is a distinct possibility that he has either been kidnapped or has faked his own disappearance. Obviously, when we are talking about the country's most senior nuclear scientist going missing, there are huge security implications. Roadblocks are being set up and ports and airports being searched. We are going to be questioning staff on the railway and residents who live alongside it. For anyone who doesn't know, the miniature railway runs all the way from Heath to Downsend, and a lot of it passes by at the bottom of people's gardens. The incident took place in open countryside, which is why the Met will be assisting us with their dog handling units."

Another murmur went round the room.

"Unfortunately it gets dark around 7 o'clock so they won't get much ground covered today. So tomorrow morning I want us all packed and ready to leave at 6am in reception, and we'll be bussed out to Downsend. Now does anyone have any questions?"

A female officer raised her hand.

"Do we know how long the enquiries are going to take, sir?"

Some of her colleagues gave her a withering look.

"Well obviously, if the Professor suddenly turns up in the middle of Tesco's wondering what all the fuss is about, not very long."

The room laughed and the officer looked embarrassed.

"No sorry, that's a fair point. I know you've all got responsibilities outside of the job, and some of you will have to make child-care arrangements and what-not. I wish I knew the answer myself, but I would definitely say a week to begin with, and if no sign of the Professor is found, maybe longer. Sorry I can't say further than that."

There were no more questions from the floor, but a few officers stayed behind to give their excuses for not being able to relocate to Downsend for the foreseeable future. The DCI had also asked Sergeant Janice Goldsmith and DS Stephen Dunwoody to wait behind for further instructions.

"Janice, I'd like you to get onto Resourcing and purloin twenty laptops; cleaned, up and running and here for tomorrow morning, can I leave that with you?

"Yes, sir, no problem." Sergeant Janice Goldsmith immediately set to work.

DCI Willis' deputy, DS Stephen Dunwoody, was known as "Woody". Willis turned to him.

"I'd like to get a head start on the investigation before tomorrow, if I can. What I'd like to know is what the Professor's mobile number was and where the last signal was traced to, or with any luck is still transmitting from. There's going to be a lot of duplication of work, inevitably, but I think it's as good a place to start as any. Will you see to that for me, Woody?"

"Yes sir. Better to have duplication than somebody missing something important."

"Precisely. Now, the first thing we need to do tomorrow is interview all the witnesses and take statements from them."

"I believe Romsey Police have already done that."

"So do I. But there's no harm in us interviewing them again 24 hours later, maybe they'll tell us something new that they have remembered overnight; that's often the way with witnesses. Do we know the name of the train driver at the time?"

Woody checked the information received from Romsey Police.

"Yes, a Mr Leonard Sutton."

"Good. Right, well, I think Len Sutton is as good a person to start with as any."

"Yes, sir."

"Okay, I'll see you tomorrow morning, then. Let's just hope the poor sod is still alive," were the Inspector's final words on the subject.

CHAPTER SIX
Len's Story

LEN SUTTON was 66 years old and had always been a fan of railways, big and small, since he was a boy. He and his wife, Alice, had rubbed along together happily enough but since they moved into their small bungalow in Romsey Sands in 1985 the spark had gone from their marriage. Len would be the first to admit that his liking for railways had quickly turned into an obsession, what with the railway line running along the bottom of his garden and the trains passing by every hour or so. He had immediately volunteered his services at the depot in New Romsey, and had progressed from ticket seller, guard and then driver over the years. As his enthusiasm for the railway grew, his marriage waned. Finally, to his mortification, Alice declared that Len was "boring" and she was leaving him for Dennis, a widower from Deal who liked *Ceroc* and had his own boat and sea-front bungalow.

Since that time two years ago, the RHLR railway had become his lifeline. His friends at the railway had been very supportive, and more than a few had been through the same thing themselves. But as well as watching the trains at the bottom of his garden, Len had another hobby; a big underground bunker affectionately known as "The Shed". This contained a second world war pumping station designed to supply oil via underground pipelines to British troops in France. It had been built as part of the PLUTO project – Pipe Lines Under The Ocean – disguised in the gardens of bungalows along the coast which had been designed to look like normal residential homes. After the war most of these bunkers had been filled in and the houses sold, but for some reason his bunker had remained intact and was now his cellar hobby room.

The first thing that Len had done when Alice left him was to add a conservatory to the rear of his bungalow over the top of his Shed's entrance. This was, firstly, because it would have annoyed the hell out of her and secondly, he could use his bolthole day or night, whatever the weather. It had been set up with a three piece suite, flatscreen tv, dartboard and a small bar which he had lit up with fairy lights for effect. He even had a CCTV camera connected to the front door and a light which would flash if anybody rang the bell.

The Shed had become a popular meeting ground for his friends from the railway, and it was where the kidnap idea had been conceived. For weeks the local papers had been full of news about the latest plans for Downsend being used as a nuclear store-room for the whole country's nuclear waste. Len had spread them out over the table in his shed for his friends to pore over.

"You can't tell me they can build that without digging up the railway as well as most of Romsey Marsh," Len grumbled.

"Bloody typical!" spat Henry, New Romsey's Senior Guard. "First it was the airport threatening to shut us down, then it was the wind farm, and now this."

"We was here first!" shouted Alan. "It stands to reason, we should be protected, just like Windsor Castle and Stonehenge. Just because we appeal to the common man, they don't think we're important enough."

"We'll show them!" Roy agreed, "We can't let them get away with it without a fight."

The fifth member of the group, Derek, jumped up at the mention of the word 'fight'. He had been an amateur boxer in his heyday, and knew how to deliver a knock-out punch.

"They'd better not show their face at the railway!" he declared, sparring into the air.

After they had finally left, Len had gone to bed that night feeling more positive than he had in months. His mind wandered again to Alice. It still rankled him that she had called him boring. Just because he didn't like the same things as she did. He imagined Alice's face seeing him being interviewed on television as a local celebrity.

"You'll be sorry then," he said quietly. "I'll show you who's boring."

The next day, by coincidence, Len had been the driver on duty when Dr Wells had turned up with his family, who had paid for him to have a Driver's Day Experience. He had been nice enough, although obviously a bit the worse for wear with drink, and had told Len that the Railway would be having an important visitor the following Friday morning.

"Well we've had the Queen," Len remarked, humouring him, "It can't be more important than that."

Dr Wells had pulled a face as if to say, "What do you know?", until Len had said, "Go on then, who is it?"

"I shouldn't be telling you this, but it's one of our most senior scientists, come to look round the plant."

"Really?" Len replied, sounding interested, "is it something to do with what was in the papers?"

"Can't tell you that," Dr Wells replied, tapping the side of his nose but smiling as if Len was right.

After this interesting afternoon Len had convened another meeting with Alan, Henry, Roy and Derek in his shed, and they all agreed that they were going to make a stand and not let this scientist's meeting take place. As the drink-fuelled evening wore on they had hatched a plan about kidnapping the scientist and keeping him locked up until the government or somebody, somewhere, guaranteed that the railway was going to be kept safe for future generations to enjoy.

The five had made certain they were on duty all day on the Friday. Len was going to be the driver of the *Green*

Dawn, as they thought this was a suitably ironic name for what they had in mind.

"The Railway's revenge," he had laughed.

Henry would be on duty as the Guard during the day, while Alan and Roy would hang around in the railway café, where they knew there was no CCTV, waiting for the signal that their target/victim had been spotted, before entering via a side-gate to the railway platform, again avoiding the CCTV cameras.

The gang had already chosen the best spot for the kidnap to occur. On Friday morning, Derek had cut a farmer's fence alongside the track and Roy had parked his van in the lane by the next field. Derek then spent the morning shoo-ing the sheep away from the hole in the wire until he had received the signal from Henry about the target boarding the train, which gave him approximately 30 minutes to drive as many sheep as possible onto the track. It was then down to Len to blow his horn loudly and as often as possible once the train came to a halt.

It had all worked like a dream, but now that they had the Professor they realised that they weren't really sure what to do next.

CHAPTER SEVEN
The Search Begins

WHEN the terrified Professor regained consciousness he found himself in a large, dilapidated caravan. He had been laid on the floor in the lounge area and three men wearing Guy Fawkes masks were sitting on some tartan built-in seats looking down at him. The room was lit with a bare light bulb and the curtains had been drawn. He began to struggle and realised that he had been bound and gagged very thoroughly. He was also no longer wearing his glasses. The Professor started to panic and this brought on an asthma attack, with him wheezing and going red in the face. His captors looked at each other.

"What shall we do?" asked the first captor.

Another man bent down and removed the gag from the professor's mouth.

"My – inhaler – jacket pocket." He spat out the words just as he began to drift back into unconsciousness. The Professor felt hands reaching inside his pockets which finally found his inhaler. Then a man took the cap off and squeezed it into his mouth. The Professor inhaled deeply.

"More?" asked the man, who sounded concerned.

The Professor nodded, and the man repeated the procedure until he finally caught his breath and began breathing normally.

"What - do - you - want - with - me?" he rasped.

"Quiet!" ordered the first captor. "You'll find out soon enough."

Professor Hills looked round in a blind panic for his briefcase, and saw that it was lying unopened on a table in the corner.

"Help! Call the Police!" he called out, as loud as his asthma would allow.

"Do you want this back in your mouth?" asked the first captor.

Professor Hills fell silent and noted that his head was throbbing violently. Despite the mask, he recognised the first captor as the one who had dealt him a knock-out blow to his forehead. He assumed him to be an expert hit-man, although the others appeared more out of shape and elderly. The hit-man then indicated to the others to go outside, where he heard them whispering to each other.

The Professor tried to make sense of his situation. The men appeared to be English, and for that he was inordinately grateful. When they had first grabbed him and pulled him out of the train carriage he had assumed they were foreign agents. But he realised that at all costs he had to prevent them from opening his briefcase, as that would make his situation immeasurably worse.

After a while, two of them came back inside the caravan and he heard a vehicle being driven away outside. They were still wearing their masks; however, he relaxed when he saw that the hit-man was no longer with them.

"Would you like a drink of water?" asked one of the men kindly.

"Yes please," he replied.

He took a few gulps, before risking a question again. "Why am I here?"

"Sorry, Professor, but we had to stop you going to that meeting," another replied.

The Professor fell silent again. He realised that they knew who he was. It could be because his name was embossed on his briefcase, but it also sounded ominously as if they knew something they shouldn't. After a few more minutes' silence, he spoke again.

"They'll come looking for me."

There was no response. After a while one of the men's mobile phones rang, and he went outside to answer it. The

Professor strained his ears but could not hear what was said. After a few minutes the man came back inside.

"Shall I bathe your head?" asked the other man, while attempting to place the Professor's glasses on.

He was surprised by this question, but replied, "Why don't you untie my hands, then I can do it myself."

The two men looked at each other and then one of them undid the rope around his wrists.

"Don't try to escape," he warned him.

"Okay," he nodded in agreement.

The Professor was relieved to be able to use his hands and swiftly used his inhaler again. After that he felt the lump on his forehead. It was the size of a duck egg, but could not feel any blood. He also realised, with horror, that his mobile phone was missing. He was still tied round the ankles, so would not be able to walk very far if he tried to escape.

The third man went into one of the bedrooms and retrieved a towel, which he soaked in some cold water in the kitchen sink before handing it to him. The Professor winced as he applied it to his head, but it was a relief to feel the cooling effect of the cold water. As he held the compress he saw for the first time the watch on his arm. It read 2.30. He had boarded the train at 12.30, so this was two hours later. He must have been unconscious for a couple of hours. In that time he could have been driven miles away from where he was kidnapped.

Professor Hills studied his captors carefully. It was obvious that these were the two men that had got out of the carriage in front of his and stood each side of his compartment. One had even asked politely, '*Can you get out, please?*' and he had almost obliged them, thinking perhaps there was a fault on the train and they needed his help. But then the third man had arrived waving a shepherd's crook through the open window in his face and demanding that he get out, before sliding the door open and dragging him out onto the track. He had just managed to grab his briefcase before this man had punched him and knocked him out cold.

If the third man had been the brawn of the group then maybe these two were the brains, although they had not shown much sign of it yet. One was completely bald and paunchy, breathing almost as heavily as he was, while the other had grey hair and was slim apart from a beer belly. He tried to remember the images of their faces into his mind and superimpose them onto the masks. One thing was for sure, he would never forget the face of his attacker, the third man, mask or not. Hills was almost tempted to tell the heavy-breathing kidnapper that he might as well take his mask off, but thought better of it.

"I need the toilet," he told them.

There was an awkward silence.

"Okay," said the bald man, "we'll help you up, but we're not going to untie your legs."

"And don't lock the door or do anything stupid," said the grey haired one.

The two of them pulled him to his feet and he hopped to the toilet door. Once inside he sat down on the toilet and considered what to do next.

"I haven't hopped for over 50 years, but I'd better get the hang of it if I'm going to escape," he thought to himself. Pulling at the rope round his legs, he managed to loosen it slightly. That was a good plan; perhaps later he could manage to work it off one foot at least, even if they tied his hands back up. After a few minutes there was a knock on the door.

"Can you come back out now?"

Hills flushed the chain and then hopped back outside. The bald man indicated that he should sit on the settee.

"How long are you going to keep me here?" he demanded.

"As long as it takes," replied the bald man.

"It's no good you asking us questions, we haven't decided," replied the other.

A few more minutes of silence went past, and Professor Hills began to concentrate on listening to his surroundings. Although he couldn't see outside, he could hear birds singing and lambs baa-ing nearby, so it sounded like they were in the middle of the countryside. He was beginning to feel even more despondent when his ears picked up the noise of something else making its way towards them. He suddenly realised it was the sound of a steam engine puffing its way past the caravan. As if to emphasise the point, it blew its whistle twice as it passed by.

"Delilah," said the grey haired man, and the other one nodded. Then they stared at the Professor, realising that he had heard it too.

A surge of relief went through Professor Hill's body. At least they hadn't taken him very far. And if he managed to escape tonight he could follow the railway line all the way to Downsend. He also realised that these men must be locals if they knew the name of the steam engine that had just gone past. That didn't suggest to him that they were international master minds. With those thoughts in mind, he began to relax.

At around 5pm a vehicle drove outside the caravan and pulled to a halt. Hills noted that it sounded different to the one before. The car beeped its horn and the two captors looked at each other and both went outside, leaving him to his own devices. The Professor immediately bent down and began loosening the rope around his ankles. After a good five minutes of struggling, he managed to untie it and slip it off his feet. He listened carefully. He heard raised voices, as if they were having an argument. Quietly, he moved from the living room into the rear of the caravan. He crept down onto the floor, then peered cautiously through the back window. All that he could see were trees and grass, with some fields in the distance. If he was right, the noise of the train had come from that direction. The men were still talking around the other side of the caravan. Carefully he tried the lever on the window, which he managed to open quietly. He realised that the window opened outwards from the bottom, and that it might be possible to squeeze through it and drop down to the ground.

Just then the door of the caravan opened and one of the men called out, "Professor, would you like a sandwich? Oh, bloody hell!" Then the bedroom door opened and the two men were pulling him back inside, while he tried to kick out at them.

"He's trying to escape!" the bald man cried out.

The third man, his attacker, suddenly appeared round the corner of the caravan and began pushing him back inside. He realised that he was outnumbered and crawled back in again, almost in tears.

"Let me go!" he shouted.

Then Alan and Roy dragged him back into the living room and the third man quickly came back inside. In the scuffle the Professor managed to pull the masks from the two men's faces and snap the elastic. Derek hadn't bothered to put his mask on at all.

They held him down as Derek tied his hands and feet back up. Meanwhile the Professor continued shouting for help.

"Who untied him?" asked Derek, annoyed.

"I did, he needed the toilet," replied Alan.

"Shout all you like, there's no-one to hear you!" Derek told him. When he was satisfied that the man was tied securely again, all three went outside again.

Inside the car sat Len and Henry, with worried expressions on their faces.

"You didn't hit him again, did you?" asked Len.

"Nah, didn't need to," Derek replied. "He won't untie himself this time."

"He's seen our faces now," said Roy. "Mind you, he would have seen them anyway when we took him."

"Well as I was saying," Henry continued, "the Police came and asked for the CCTV video. And then I had to make a statement explaining what happened today and what the two men looked like who got in the carriage in front of him."

"What did you say?" asked Alan anxiously.

"I said they were two short dark men with foreign accents, maybe Turkish."

"I got quizzed at Downsend as well," said Len. "I told them that I never saw anything."

"What about me?" asked Derek.

"Oh yes, they did ask me if I saw the farmer. I said, only briefly; it was a tall man wearing jeans and a fleece but I couldn't give much of a description other than that."

"Oh thank you!" said Derek sarcastically. "That sounds like me and I *am* wearing jeans and a fleece."

"Don't forget they are going to interview the passengers as well," Len replied.

"Oh dear," said Henry, "I hadn't thought of that."

Just at that moment a large whirring sound distracted them, and they looked up in amazement as first one and then two Chinook helicopters flew directly overhead. They watched as the machines headed in the direction of Downsend.

"Bloody hell!" exclaimed Alan. "You don't think they are looking for the Professor, do you?"

Len shrugged.

"Put the news on," ordered Roy.

Len switched his car radio on, which was tuned to the local channel. After 30 seconds of music there came a news bulletin.

"Just to update you on some breaking news, the police have asked the public for any information they may have on the missing Professor Mark Hills, who was last seen on the 12.30 Romsey Heath and Little Church miniature railway heading towards Downsend. The Police have requested that people search their sheds and outbuildings for signs of anything untoward and to report anything unusual they may have witnessed in the surrounding area. We will update you on this fast moving story on the six o'clock news."

"So he's called 'Mark'. That makes him more human somehow," Henry noted.

"We're going to have to be very careful," said Len thoughtfully. "Alan and Roy, don't say anything to the missus."

"As if I'd tell her indoors anything, it would be all over the country by the morning," Alan joked.

"I'd trust Carol with my life," Roy stated. "But no, it wouldn't be fair on her, she might not agree with it."

Derek and Henry were both single, like Len.

"How long are we going to keep him, anyway?" Roy persisted.

"Well, we need to make a point. It's no good letting him go right away, that won't do any good. We have to let him know the reason why we've done it, and see what he says. If he goes along with it, we can let him go earlier. If he doesn't agree, well –"

"Well, what?" quizzed Henry.

"Well, I suppose we will have to make our point a bit more forcefully."

Derek laughed, then said, "What about the practicalities? We've still got to feed and water him, and he's going to need some clothes."

Len looked at Derek.

"Good point. You're about the same height as him, you must have some old clothes he can use. Alan and Roy, you're going to have to go home each night as normal, but you can still take turns keeping an eye on him during the day. I'm thinking we may need to hold onto him for a week, at most. I don't see any point in detaining him for longer."

"We could all be going to prison," remarked Derek. "He's seen our faces, it's only fair that he sees yours and Henry's."

"Right, okay, I'm happy with that. Come on, Henry, let's go inside and talk to Mark."

They got out of their car, unpacking carrier bags containing food and drink, and all made their way back inside the caravan. They found the Professor still where Derek had left him, tied up on the floor.

The Professor looked alarmed as two new faces walked into the caravan.

"Hello, Mark, my name's Len. I expect you are wondering why you are here?"

The Professor looked back with real fear in his eyes.

"You are here because all of us are fighting for something we really believe in – the Railway."

"The railway?" The Professor could not keep the surprise from his voice.

"Yes, the Railway. It's very important to us that the Romsey, Heath and Little Church Railway is preserved for future generations."

"So what has that got to do with me?"

"Because your lot think they own Romsey Marsh and can do what they like with it!" roared Derek.

"Yes, bloody dig it up and build all over it. Never mind about the railway and all the people who depend on it," added Alan.

"Well, if it's jobs you are worried about, I'm sure there would be plenty..." the Professor's voice faltered.

"That's not the attitude, Professor," said Len.

"You just don't get it, do you?" said Alan. "It's not just about jobs, it's a way of life. We love it!"

"It's somewhere for us to go, to feel useful," added Henry.

"There's nothing else round here, one bus an hour if you're lucky. The kids have to use the train to get to school," said Alan.

"My old mother uses it to do her shopping," Roy chipped in.

"We was here first!" Alan stated.

They all looked at the Professor, waiting for his reply. He could feel the sweat running down his brow.

"Look, I'm sorry that your railway runs through one of the most sensitive sites in the country. Perhaps they could move it?"

"What, the plant?" asked Roy.

"He means the railway," said Len.

The men all glared fiercely back at the Professor, who decided silence was the best option.

"Well we can't let him go anywhere with ideas like that," Len said to the group. The other men agreed.

"No bloody coronation chicken sandwiches for you, you can have the plain cheese," said Alan, throwing some pre-packed sandwiches into Mark's lap.

The others laughed as Alan distributed the food around. They watched as the Professor fumbled to open the sandwich packet with his wrists tied, but was unable to.

"Just a minute, I'll untie you," said Len, bending down to help. He then opened a can of coke and passed it to him.

"Why don't we switch on the telly, we might get some more information," Henry suggested. Derek turned it on and tuned it to the news channel, which led the Professor to believe that it must be his caravan. The national news was in progress.

"Our reporter, Lorraine Wilkes, is on the scene. Is there anything more you can tell us?"

"Well, Simon, I'm in a place known locally as 'Jackson's Farm' which is in-between St. Joseph's Bay and New Romsey and, as you can see behind me, teams of police dogs are scouring the countryside around this area to search for any trace of Professor Hills, the man who has gone missing. The exact circumstances surrounding the Professor's disappearance are unclear, however it appears that he boarded the 12.30 miniature railway heading for Downsend but he never arrived. Now we understand that Professor Hills was due to attend a meeting at Downsend Power Station to discuss possible options for the future of the plant, which is due to be decommissioned."

The screen changed to show police officers questioning drivers.

"That's by Monty's field!" exclaimed Alan.

"Shush!" Len ordered.

"Police have also set up roadblocks in both directions and vehicles are being stopped and in some cases searched."

"Have the police issued any statements, Lorraine?"

"Yes, they have. As you can see, the area around here is pretty remote, with lots of farms and outbuildings, and the Police are requesting members of the public, including farmers, to check their sheds, barns and caravans for signs that anyone may be living in them or for any unusual activity to call this number: 0800-711-999, or call Crimestoppers on 0800-555-111anonymously, if they prefer.

Now the authorities are taking this incident very seriously indeed, even as a matter of national security, and a few minutes ago two Chinook helicopters passed overhead en-route to Downsend filled, we believe, with personnel drafted in to assist the investigation."

"Thanks very much, Lorraine. We will be providing updates throughout the evening as this situation progresses, but for now on with other news..."

Derek turned the television off, to a momentary stunned silence.

"I told you they'd come looking for me," said the Professor.

"Everyone back outside," ordered Len.

"I'm tying him up first," said Derek.

They waited while he tied the Professor's wrists. The men were now extremely worried by what they had seen.

"They're less than a mile away," hissed Derek.

"I know, and there's road blocks," Len replied.

"We've got the bloody SAS onto us, as well," Alan remarked, referring to the helicopters.

"We can't leave him here, if they don't find him tonight they'll find him in the morning," said Henry.

"I know that, I'm trying to think of something," replied Len.

"There's only one way out of here now," said Roy.

They all turned and looked at him.

"The railway."

Len looked around the group and they all nodded in agreement.

"Right then, on to Plan B," Len replied.

"There is no Plan B," said Derek.

"Yes there is – the Shed!"

CHAPTER EIGHT
Vintage Weekend

PETER MASON was facing a huge dilemma. It was only 8.00 o'clock in the morning and already he had spoken with Craig, the Metropolitan Police Dog Division, Romsey Police, the Leader of Romsey Council and the owners of RHLR. The problem was that the railway were holding a special event, *Vintage Weekend*, this Saturday and Sunday. Craig was in favour of cancellation, pointing out that armed personnel were searching all the properties between Downsend and Heath alongside the railway track. The Dog Division had also made a valid case that the *Vintage Weekend* should be cancelled. For one thing, thousands of people wandering about the countryside might destroy any scent trails that the dogs may find and for another, innocent people may get followed or even bitten by any dogs off the lead.

Romsey Police had taken a more pragmatic view that it was too late in the day to cancel the event and they felt they had enough officers, including military personnel, to keep all the stations guarded in case the Professor should show up. The Council Leader had also begged for the RHLR event to remain open as it was a huge boost to tourism in the area, and jobs depended on events such as this to support the fairly poor local economy. Of course, the Romsey, Heath & Little Church Railway were the most vociferous in their objections to a cancellation. They pointed out that 40 coachloads of visitors were known to be travelling up even as they spoke for the occasion, from destinations as far away as Cornwall and Sheffield, who had all paid to attend the event and the Sunday barbecue, before leaving on Sunday night. This meant that around 1,600 people had made hotel bookings for the weekend, as well as the thousands of people who were making daytrips or had organised displays such as classic vehicle shows, complete with vintage costumes.

Mason sighed. He'd had a heavy evening the night before with his daughter, although she had eventually agreed to go for a drink, where she vented her ever-present anger. Now he was responsible for a decision which could annoy some very high-up people, including his Deputy, or disappointing thousands of innocent bystanders. Mason thought that a compromise could be reached. If the RHLR would agree that nobody was allowed to wander off site at their stations or get on or off at Downsend, maybe the weekend could be saved. Surely the combined security services had enough men shipped down there to stand guard and make sure this happened? Added to which, it was a chance for his plain-clothed operatives to mingle with the crowds and get a feel for the local area, which could prove very useful. Decision made, he then had the task of relaying it to the persons involved. Not a great start to the day, and compromises rarely pleased anyone, in his experience. If he'd made the wrong choice, he would have to resign.

Craig, meanwhile, had been focusing his attention on the Professor's mobile phone and whether it was still producing a signal. He had also ordered a breakdown of Dr Wells' telephone calls over the last three months. At around 10 a.m. he received some good news. The mobile had last emitted a signal from an area of farmland known locally as 'Monty's fields', and he immediately telephoned the Metropolitan Police dog units and requested that they search that area.

"Yes, sir, I do believe they are already in the area," came the response.

"That's fortunate," Craig responded.

The person on the other line paused. "We were actually asked to go there by DCI Willis of Sussex HQ," the officer replied.

"Oh, I see." Craig was non-plussed. "Well can you make sure that if you find anything, I am the first person to know about it?" he asked, trying to keep the annoyance from his voice.

"Certainly, sir," they responded.

Craig hung up the telephone and considered what he had been told. He could not understand how DCI Willis could have got this information before he had. Then he remembered that Willis and his team were heading for Downsend this morning and were expected any minute now. Craig realised that he had not made room in his HQ for another twenty people, plus computers and desks, and cursed to himself. DCI Willis was already getting on his nerves.

"Ben! Chris! Can you find another twenty desks from somewhere and place them at the back of the hall?"

"And chairs as well, sir?"

"Yes, of course."

Just at that moment Craig spotted a middle-aged, unfit man being directed towards him by one of his men. He moved towards him.

"DCI Willis? Good morning, I'm Craig Bennett, MI8."

The men shook hands.

"Nice to meet you. Please call me Simon. Ah, this is a nice little set-up." DCI Willis appraised the room, admiring the neat rows of desks and computers, with men diligently tapping on their keypads. He looked puzzled. "I don't see anywhere for my team to sit?"

Craig flushed. "We're just sorting that for you now, Simon."

"Oh, I see. Right. Only they want to start work straight away, you know how it is. Is there a staff canteen, by any chance?"

"Well yes, but I don't think it's open."

"That's fine, we'll all go and sit in there and you can let us know when the room is ready."

Craig could feel his hackles rising. "I'll certainly get somebody to call you, yes."

"Thank you, much appreciated. And getting back to basics, I will need a telephone line. Is there one set up in here?"

"Yes, on my desk." Craig pointed to a single telephone sitting on his desk at the front of the hall.

"I see. Well, I'm going to need one of them too. Whom should I ask about that?"

"Don't worry, I'll see to it," Craig replied, through gritted teeth.

"Much obliged, thank you. Okay, well I'll get my team sorted out and then maybe we can have a catch up later this morning?"

The other man grunted and walked off.

"Woody!" The Inspector finally found his deputy. "Can you round all the men – and woman – up and direct them to the canteen?"

"Oh, is that going to be our office, then?"

"For now, yes. It's got tables and chairs and food on tap; sounds about perfect to me."

"When you put it like that I agree, sir. See you in there." Woody rushed back outside to round up his team, who had disembarked from a bus hired for the occasion. Even though there were only fifteen of them it had been a squeeze, with all carrying laptops and suitcases full of clothing.

The Inspector waited until all his team had raided the vending and coffee machines and had seated themselves in rows in the middle of the canteen. Only fifteen of his officers had been able to commit to a week away from home, but more could be seconded in if necessary.

"Okay, everybody, I'm just going to have a brief catch-up with you all. I'll fill you in this afternoon with more information, if I have any. Now as some of you know, the missing Professor's phone last emitted a signal at 8 p.m. last night in an area near New Romsey known as "Monty's Fields". The Met dog units are out there now searching for it, just in case it is still there. We can't rely on that, though, so we are still going to be searching the whole of the area from Heath to Downsend. Our brief is to knock on people's doors and take statements from all the residents along the railway line, asking whether they heard or saw anything unusual last Friday or since then – you know, people acting suspiciously, any foreigners with strange accents they may have noticed. This isn't London, so foreign accents are still unusual."

The team laughed.

"There's a few areas I'm unsure about, for example, the holiday camp at Romsey Sands. I'm assuming those units will have to be searched and any holidaymakers interviewed, but I need to clarify that with Mr Bennett. He's the man in charge of the MI8 investigation, by the way. Can I ask that you cooperate with him just as you would me?"

The team replied "yes".

"Okay, what we have so far are seven statements from witnesses to the events. That being the train driver, Mr Len Sutton; the Guard, Henry Smith, and seven passengers, including two being young boys. They are very short statements of fact, and my intention is that we get more detailed statements from them and an identikit drawn up of the potential suspects in the train carriage immediately in front of the Professor. These two men have still not made themselves known, so they are definitely persons of interest. Janice, have you printed off the copies of these statements?"

"Yes, sir. Shall I hand them out?"

"If you would. So, working in teams of two I'd like you to interview each of the witnesses again, and report back this afternoon with any updates and an identikit. The address of each witness and their phone number is given on their statement on the printout."

"The problem with the description of the suspects, sir," Janice prompted.

"Oh yes, thanks for reminding me. One thing we need to clarify is the description of these two missing passengers. The guard described them as swarthy, short and stocky with foreign accents, possibly Turkish. The female witness, Irene Tremayne, gave a different account. She said that one was bald and quite overweight whilst the other was tall and skinny. We are also seeking a third man, who purported to be the farmer of the stray sheep, described as tall, dark and muscular, wearing a fleece. He is also a suspect so I'd like an identikit of him, as well. He is the only person that all the witnesses on the train got some kind of look at. The sooner we can issue identikit pictures to the press, the better. Okay, is everyone clear on what they are doing?"

"Yes, sir."

Woody stepped forward. "I believe the railway is running a special event over the weekend, so the driver and the guard will probably be working on the railway."

"Good point, Woody, thank you. Well I'll let you enjoy your breakfast and then decide between you who is working together and which witness you are interviewing. Woody is going to help me coordinate the Inquiry here. Hopefully, we'll have a bit of space in the main HQ for when you get back this afternoon. I'll meet you in there at 1 o'clock. Is everybody clear on what they are doing now?"

"Yes, sir," came the response.

Woody finally chose some food from the vending machine and sat next to his boss. The sandwiches looked a bit suspect, being left over from the day before. He opened the packet slowly and opened the sandwich, unsure whether to eat the rubbery looking cheese slice or not. The Inspector decided not to voice his opinion on the matter.

"I wonder how Romsey Police got on with the CCTV recording?" he mused.

"Shall I ring them now?"

"No, no, eat your breakfast first. But that recording should have captured the two suspects before they boarded the train. That would help us decide which description to build the identikits on."

"I'll get onto them as soon as I've eaten this."

"No immediate rush, Woody." He lowered his voice. "Have you noticed that Janice is the only female of any description in the building?"

"No, sir, I haven't really looked."

"Well she's the only one in our team that could take the week away from home, and I didn't see a single woman in HQ."

"Really? I'll have to check."

"Only, thing is, I'd prefer you kept her out on the road rather than being gawped at in here all day."

"Right, I'll make sure I do that."

DCI Willis munched on his cold bacon roll thoughtfully. He didn't want there to be any shenanigans on his watch. It was too easy as a police officer to get involved in an affair, due to the stresses and the long hours away from home. He knew that through his own personal experience. He was on his second marriage to Eileen, who was also a serving police officer. It seemed that was the only way to a happy relationship – to find somebody who truly understood the pressures of the job and accepted the working all hours at short notice.

After half an hour the officers teamed up and were busy making appointments to visit their various witnesses, and Woody went outside to telephone Romsey Police. After a few minutes he rushed back to find his boss, who was outside the HQ peering in to see if his desk had been set up.

"Sir, I've got an update on the CCTV."

"Great, any sign of the suspects on there?"

"No, and that is very strange. The officers have viewed all of the CCTV from 9 o'clock, when the front door was opened, until the train left at 12.30. They've got a good view of the Professor and all of the other passengers in the shop buying their tickets, but not the two men we are looking for."

"That's really odd. Is there any way the men could have boarded the train without buying a ticket or passing through the shop?"

"No, sir. Not according to the Station Master. The only other way in is through the side gate, which has a keypad lock on the front so you would need to know the code."

"So what did the Guard say; did he sell the men any tickets, or did they already have one?"

"That would be Henry Smith. He doesn't remember selling them any tickets. He's the one who described them as short and dark, possibly Turkish."

"Well there's something suspicious about all of that, don't you think?"

"Yes, sir."

"And I suppose the only people who would know the whereabouts of the CCTV cameras would be people who worked there, unless the place had been scouted beforehand." DCI Willis rubbed his chin thoughtfully. "I'm wondering whether it could be an inside job."

"It would make sense, sir; somebody who knew the area and the trains, to pull off such a crime."

"Hmm. What does our driver, Mr Sutton, have to say?"

Woody rifled through the statements.

"He said he didn't see the two men getting on the train."

"That's rather convenient. Remind me about the third man, the one who was supposed to be a farmer, how does Mr Sutton describe him?"

"Tall, dark and muscular, wearing a fleece."

"And that's the same as the other witness statements, is it?"

"I think so." Woody checked quickly through the statements, looking for the yellow highlighting." "Yes, more or less."

"All right, Woody, can I leave you to check on the background of Mr Smith – if that's his real name. Just a thought, it might be an idea to ask the Station Master to provide photos of all the staff who work there, and then the team can show those to the witnesses. Perhaps you can ask them to hold fire until then. I might even ask our friend, Craig, if he can help us with some surveillance. Let's see if you've got a desk, first."

The two men wandered inside the HQ and surveyed the scene. It appeared that some desks had been lined up against the back wall and down the left hand side, which Willis assumed were for his team.

"I suppose these are ours. Not a very practical layout, but we only really need somewhere to rest our laptops at the end of a day's work. I'm planning to make sure the team are out on the road for 90 per cent of the time anyway, taking witness statements."

"Right, I'll just go and retrieve my suitcase from the canteen. I've written down who is interviewing who in there." Woody wandered off again.

There was still no telephone line set up, as far as DCI Willis could tell. That was essential for his way of working. Mobiles might be a great invention, but he had never got the knack of holding one in the crook of his neck while he wrote things down in a notebook. They also had a tendency to get uncomfortably hot after a few minutes. He spotted Craig talking to somebody and headed over in the same direction. Craig paused, and the other man hurried away.

"Hello Craig, thanks for setting the desks up, that looks ideal."

The younger man smiled, in spite of himself. The Inspector noted that he was really quite insecure, which made him somewhat defensive.

"Oh yes, we're having a bit of trouble getting a telephone line in, it might not be ready until tomorrow now. You know what it's like at weekends with the telecoms people."

"I do indeed. Maybe there's another office somewhere that I can use in the mean time?"

"Well… there's always the Commander's office, until he gets here. It's a bit more private."

"Who, sorry?"

"My boss, Peter Mason."

"Oh, I see. Well, that would be very useful, if he doesn't mind. Maybe we could have a little catch up meeting in there now, if you're free?"

"Right. Okay, of course. I'll just get my briefcase. Be right back."

The Inspector also retrieved his case and wheeled it back to Craig, who was indicating towards a small room next to the HQ.

"In here, sir."

"Thanks. Call me Simon, please," he said again.

The Inspector looked round the tiny room containing one desk and a telephone. "This will be perfect for now, just what I need. I wanted to have a little catch up with you on any developments in the case."

"Right. What, now?"

"If you wouldn't mind."

Willis followed Craig inside the room and closed the door, waiting for him to begin.

"Okay. We're focusing mainly on known foreign agents, and we are trying to trace their whereabouts last Friday. We've also got several governments very interested in what's happening, so we have to keep them updated."

"I'll bet they are. Can you remind me again how old the Professor is?"

"Just had his 55th birthday."

"Prime time for an emotional meltdown, then. Because I've got the impression that there's a possibility the Professor may have 'disappeared' intentionally. Is that still the case?"

"Well between you and me, I don't think so." Craig tried to convey that this was a bluff to the DCI by giving him his '*I can't say any more*' stare. Willis looked momentarily puzzled.

"Oh, I see. I won't bother to ask about his family, then. I just wondered if everything was fine at home, that's all."

"He was divorced, no known girlfriend that we can find. Not even anything untoward on his computer."

"What, not even any porn? Most unusual. What about his financial position?"

"He wasn't exactly wealthy, having just put his sons through University. But he has no bad credit history or debts that we can find."

"Right, well I'll concentrate on my first thoughts then, that this was an inside job."

Craig looked astonished. MI8 were using their finest minds to track down any foreign involvement and this Copper was hinting at a little local set-up. Which, to be fair, his boss had also suggested concerning Dr Wells.

"I see. Well if – if you need any help..." he stuttered.

"Actually, I was going to ask you a favour. We haven't got the resources to do any surveillance, unfortunately, and I wondered if you could spare a few of your men to keep an eye on one of the railway men, a Mr Henry Smith."

"Yes, that's what most of them are here for, covert surveillance. Can you give me his details?"

"Just a moment." Willis opened the door and called in Woody, who had been patiently waiting outside. "Have you got Henry Smith's statement, please?"

Woody rifled through his bundle of papers and handed over Henry's statement.

"Yes, here's his address."

"Let me check my map. Follow me, gentlemen." Craig led them back to the hall and over to a large map beside his desk at the front of the HQ. "Let's see, Smallstone Road. No, we haven't reached that area yet. I can certainly get his house searched."

"Well, we don't want to do anything that might scare him," Willis replied hurriedly. "Just suppose that he has got the Professor, or knows his whereabouts, we don't want to panic them into doing anything silly. Which reminds me, have you had a ransom note yet?"

"Nothing at all, unfortunately. Apart from the mobile phone signal, we have no clues."

Willis paused. "We have found some anomalies with the witness statements and the lack of CCTV. That's why we want Mr Smith to be checked out, but covertly."

"Yes, I can arrange that. Anything else?"

"The train driver, Mr Sutton, where does he live?"

Woody checked Len's statement. "356 The Parade".

Craig checked his map. "I think that's by the seafront, and we've done that this morning. Yes, that's right. His house would have been searched."

"Right, okay, we won't worry about him for now; just Henry Smith, if you could."

"I'll see to it right away, and I'll let you know if there's any developments."

"Thanks very much, Craig."

"No problem, Simon."

The two men smiled and Craig went in search of two surveillance candidates.

"You've got him eating out of your hand," said Woody.

"It's called 'charm', Woody. How else do you think I got to where I am," he replied wryly.

CHAPTER NINE
Plan B

THE GANG waited until 10 p.m. to put their plans into place. Len drove Henry to New Romsey Station and Henry let them both in through the side gate. The building was deserted and all the trains were safely stored away in the sidings. Len and Henry knew how to drive every single one of the engines, but their plan tonight was to use the Baron Hughie diesel locomotive, being much quieter to run than a steam train. Len quickly drove it from the sidings and onto the main track, where Henry attached one carriage and a goods wagon to the back. The wagon was normally used to transport coal around the depot, but tonight this would be carrying a different kind of cargo. Both men squeezed into the front of the train and set off to their rendezvous point.

Outside of the caravan, meanwhile, a fierce debate had ensued on how to persuade the Professor to comply with their plans but, realising they were running out of time, simply added three sleeping tablets to his can of coke while he wasn't watching and waited for him to pass out. Rather that, they thought, than risk another asthma attack with a gag on.

At ten-thirty Henry rang Derek's mobile three times to let him know that they were just leaving the depot. By this time the Professor was comatose, and Derek went into action. He retrieved a blanket from one of the cupboards and wrapped it round the man, securing it with string. Alan left the caravan first and led with a torch while Derek carried the Professor over his shoulder, much like he had when they first captured him. Roy followed on behind with the suitcase, looking back often to make sure they weren't being watched.

Derek lowered the Professor gently into the rear wagon, then the three men joined the passenger compartment. Henry took over the driver's position and Len seated himself next to his friends on the train. When they had driven for another fifteen minutes Henry came to a halt. Len jumped out first and Derek helped him over his back fence, where he then ran to open his back door and pulled open the entrance to the basement. Then he grabbed a torch, hurried back to the fence and opened the gate. This had been a handy shortcut for him to get to Romsey Sands Station in the past, and he was very thankful now that he'd installed it. Derek, meanwhile, had hauled the Professor out of the goods wagon and was carrying him over his shoulder.

"Quick, inside!" Len hissed.

The moment that Derek, the Professor, Alan and Roy had entered Len's garden, Henry reversed the Baron Hughie back up the line to New Romsey. Len padlocked his gate once more and ushered them into his conservatory.

"Right, everyone down in the shed, Derek first!" he ordered.

"Mind his head!" hissed Alan, as Derek carried him down the steps and then laid him on the settee. The Professor was still sleeping soundly.

"Phew, I think I need a drink," said Len, sweating profusely.

"Me too, I've done all the hard work," Derek replied.

"I'll have to tell the missus that I'm not coming home tonight," said Roy, pulling out his mobile. "I'll just go upstairs."

The shed was lead-lined and had no mobile reception.

"Tell her you've had one too many," Len suggested.

"Ask her to let Linda know while you're at it, please," asked Alan, and added, "I think now would be a good time to open the briefcase, don't you?"

"Drinks first." Len poured his friends a drink and put one on the bar for Roy. Then he found his toolbox and got out a screwdriver. "Maybe I can unscrew the hinges on it."

Despite his best efforts, the briefcase was proving tamper-proof.

"Give it here," said Derek. He prised a flat-end screwdriver into the top of the briefcase and whacked it with a hammer, making a dent in it.

The Professor stirred.

"Shush!" ordered Len. "We'll have to do it upstairs."

He knocked down a shot of whisky and Derek did the same, before going back upstairs and closing the shed door. Loud banging and cursing could be heard until the men heard a jubilant, "That's it!"

Roy and Alan joined them as Len opened the case. They found inside stuffed full with lots of plastic wallets full of colour diagrams and a document marked "RESTRICTED – CLASSIFIED TOP SECRET".

"What do you make of all these? Looks like some kind of engine." Derek passed the diagrams to Len. He leafed through the plastic wallets and his eyes widened.

"I know a bit about engines," he replied, "and this looks like a combustion engine – a nuclear combustion engine!"

"S**t!" Alan exclaimed. "No wonder they're going hell for leather to find him, I think it's this they're really looking for."

"Now we're for it!" Len agreed. "What the hell do we do now?"

Derek looked at the paperwork again. "This is probably worth a lot of money," he remarked.

Len shook his head. "Don't even think about it! There's only one thing for it, we've somehow got to get this, and the Professor, back to Downsend in one piece."

Roy joined them and gawped in amazement at the papers spread out in Len's lounge.

"Did you hear that, Roy, Len thinks we should let the Professor go," said Alan.

"Look, these are all top secret plans!" Len explained.

"But I thought that's why we took him, ain't it, because we don't want a giant nuclear reprocessing plant built on the marsh?" Alan queried.

"Yeah, that's right," Derek agreed.

"No I don't want it, none of us wants it, but one thing I'm not is a traitor! We can't be destroying top secret plans!" Len stated angrily.

"Where's my drink?" Roy exclaimed. "I think we all need to have a drink and calm down a bit, and then we can decide what's best to do next."

They all climbed back down into the shed. The Professor was still sleeping soundly as Len put his diagrams back inside the briefcase and tried to patch it up again. Then he poured them all a stiff shot of whisky, which the men drank in silence.

"We can't take him there by van, there's roadblocks everywhere," Derek whispered.

"And we can't get him on the train in broad daylight, we'll have to wait until tomorrow night," said Roy.

The Professor was snoring loudly, still in a deep sleep.

"We can't deliver him in that state, in any case," said Len.

"I suppose we could just own up, say we've got in out of our depth?" Alan suggested.

"Oh, and we'll just get slapped wrists and told not to do it again?" said Derek sarcastically.

"Look," said Len, "we can't make any decisions without speaking to Henry. We're all in this together, and he needs to be consulted too."

"I agree," said Roy.

"He's not working tomorrow," Alan reminded them.

"Oh yes, that's right. We'll have to ring his mobile," Roy replied.

"Huh, fat chance. He's never got it switched on," Alan remarked.

"We're going to have to get our act together," said Len. "Can somebody call me tomorrow when you've managed to get hold of him?"

They all nodded in agreement.

"Right then. Well there's no point worrying about it until we've spoken to him. We might as well have another drink!" Len filled all their glasses again and they settled down for a long night, ready to help should the Professor wake up again. Derek and Len took the chairs in the shed, with Alan and Roy sleeping in the conservatory upstairs.

They were rudely awoken by the sound of the doorbell buzzing.

"What's that?" asked Derek, looking rough.

Len peered into his CCTV cameras. In the throes of a hangover, his eyes were like slits. "Oh my god, it's the Police!" he hissed. He moved as fast as he was able up the steps and into the conservatory. "Get down in the basement, quick!" he ordered.

The noise brought Derek and Alan to their senses, and they stumbled down into the basement. Luckily, the Professor had not stirred. The doorbell rang again, with more urgency. They all stared at the CCTV camera. The Police looked undecided, and one was talking into his walkie-talkie outside.

"Look, they've got a battering ram!" said Derek.

"I'll have to let them in before they break the door down!" said Len, heading for the hatch.

"No!" yelled Alan.

"It's all right, I'll pull a rug over the entrance. Just keep quiet!" Len ordered, before closing the opening. He hastily pulled the rug in the Conservatory over the Shed entrance and called out, "All right, hold on!" before rushing to the door.

Outside stood four military policeman, who looked relieved that they did not have to batter his door down. He also noticed they were armed.

"Good morning, sir." The man in front flashed Len a photopass. "You may have seen the news about the man who has gone missing from the railway that runs at the back of you?"

"Well, yes, but…"

"I'm sorry to disturb you, sir, but we have authority under the Prevention of Terrorism Act to search all properties that back on to the railway."

"I see. Of course, feel free." Len stood aside to let the four men pass. Hearing the sound of splintering wood he stepped outside and watched in amazement as his neighbour's front door was bashed in by another group of four, who then rushed inside. He knew the owners, who used the property as a holiday home and were probably in London. Len then looked up and down the street, his mouth gawping in amazement. The scene that greeted him resembled world war three. Men in combat jackets and sub-machine guns were stood in the middle of the street beside an armoured vehicle, while overhead two helicopters patrolled the coastline. Len shielded his eyes and stared out to sea at what appeared to be a battleship in the distance. Added to which, he could hear the fierce barking of what sounded like angry Alsatians heading his way.

After what seemed like ages but was only a few minutes later the four men came back out again, thanked him like he had a choice in the matter, wrote something down and crossed his address off a list. Len hurriedly shut the door behind them and stood braced against his front door, breathing heavily and stifling the desire to scream. When he had stopped hyperventilating he made his way back to the conservatory, pulled the rug aside and opened up the entrance to the shed, almost collapsing on the way down the steps as his legs turned to jelly. The three others looked equally wide-eyed and afraid by what had just happened. Speechless, Len forced himself to look across at the Professor on the couch, and had never been more glad to see a man sleeping. When he found his voice, he said shakily:

"It's like Armageddon out there. Tanks, sub-machine guns, helicopters, warships …" his voice tailed off.

"I know, we were watching on the CCTV," gasped Roy.

"What do we do now?" asked Alan wildly.

"It's no good panicking, we've got to come up with a plan," said Derek.

"Right." Len paced the room, thinking on his feet. "It's Vintage Weekend, so there's going to be a lot of people about on the railway."

"Do you think they might cancel it?" asked Alan.

"Maybe. But you've got to turn up for work anyway just in case, otherwise it'll look suspicious. I'll have to ring in sick. What time's the first train to Romsey Sands on the special timetable?"

"9.58," replied Roy.

"Oh yes, that's right, or else it's 10.58." Len looked at the clock on the wall, which read 9.30. "Let's hope the trains are still running as normal. Anyway, what I think we should do is, one of you leave every five minutes from the back gate and walk up the track to Romsey Sands station. If you catch the train, don't all sit together."

"Will you be all right with him?" asked Derek.

Len thought carefully. "I've got a bicycle chain padlock, perhaps I can chain him to the pipes."

"His hands are still tied," said Alan.

"That's good. I'll just go and get the padlock, then Derek, can you help me to sort him out?"

"Yes, no problem."

"Okay, I think you two should think about leaving." Len indicated to Roy and Alan.

Derek stayed with the Professor while the other three went upstairs. Len opened his back door cautiously and peered out, checking there were no helicopters flying overhead. Len let Roy through his back gate, before running back inside.

"Okay, leave it five minutes before you go," he told Alan, still waiting in the conservatory.

Len found his bike chain and padlock and rushed back down to the cellar.

"You'll have to help me move the sofa nearer to the machine," he instructed Derek.

The men lifted the sofa with the Professor still on it into position. He remained fast asleep, stirring occasionally. The men spoke in whispers.

"I'll put the chain round his ankle," Derek hissed, "You go and get a bottle of water and a bucket."

Len rushed to retrieve the items from the bar area.

The Professor was securely padlocked to a pipe on the old pumping machine. He now had the basics for survival; a blanket, somewhere to sleep, a bottle of water and a bucket to go to the toilet in. That would have to do until they thought of their next steps.

"If you're sure you'll be all right with him, I'll be going," said Derek.

"Okay. Let me know what Henry thinks," Len whispered, as Derek made his way up the steps.

Len listened carefully as he heard his conservatory door close. He felt suddenly very claustrophobic, stuck down here with the Professor. A few minutes later he heard the welcome sound of a steam engine thundering almost overhead as it passed by. He listened carefully to the "whooo-woo" whistle as it pulled into Romsey Sands Station, hopefully with his friends all on board.

"*Northern Squire*," he said out loud.

The Professor stirred.

"It's just you and me now, Professor," Len said quietly. "You, me, and the trains."

CHAPTER TEN
Phone Home

AT 11 o'clock on Saturday morning, Craig got the news he was waiting for.

"We've found the mobile phone, sir."

"Great stuff! Whereabouts was it?"

"In the middle of a field, in an area known as Monty's fields."

"Right. I want as many units as possible deployed to that area and to focus on any buildings within a half mile radius."

"Yes, sir. There's not much around here so that shouldn't take too long."

"Good. And if you don't find anything, increase the radius to one mile. Can somebody put the phone in an evidence bag and bring it to me at HQ asap?"

"Yes, we'll bike that to you right away. Can we request some helicopter back-up, sir?"

"Certainly. If you can give me the satellite coordinates I'll do that right away."

"Er, right. I'll have to get back to you with those."

"Okay, speak soon."

"Yes, sir, 'bye."

"Yes!" Craig exclaimed out loud. The room suddenly went quiet.

"Listen, everyone, we've found the Professor's mobile phone, so can forensics get onto that as soon as it arrives? One point to mention, I think it's highly unlikely that the Professor would have dropped his phone in the middle of a field on purpose if he had decided to do a disappearing act. This now looks almost certainly to be a kidnapping. So if you have any leads in this respect, please tell me immediately. That's all for now, thank you."

A buzz went round the hall. Two people who had been dedicated to researching the Professor's private life looked bemused as to what to do next. One of them printed off all the results on his computer and handed them over to Craig.

"These are the bank statements for the Professor, his wife and both sons. I've also printed off the websites visited by them all for the last six months. Geoff's got the Professor's mobile phone printout for the last six months, as well."

"Okay, Paul, well that's all useful information, thank you."

"Do you want me to stop working on this now?"

"Yes, I'll assign you to something else. But I'd first be interested to know the times that the Professor contacted Dr Wells, or vice versa, on that printout. I've got his number here, can you ask Geoff for a report?"

"Yes, sir."

"Okay, thanks. In fact, I'll assign you to Dr Wells now – addresses, bank accounts and websites; and perhaps Geoff can work on his mobile phone list, too."

"Yes, I'll let him know."

"Great! Can you give me an update by 1700 hours, and I'll advise Peter."

"Sir." The man nodded and went back to his desk.

"I'd better update the boss," Craig thought to himself, pushing fast dial number one. Mason picked it up immediately.

"Hello Craig, any news?"

"Hello sir, yes, we've just located Professor Hills' phone."

"Good, at last something we can work on. Where was it?"

"In the middle of a field. We're getting it biked here now."

"I see. Get it checked for prints as well, won't you?

"Yes."

"Well that ends the theory that he went wandering off, I'd say. Most likely it fell out of his pocket while he was being abducted."

"I agree."

"No word from anyone, anywhere claiming to have taken him, I suppose?"

"Not yet, sir."

"Damn! I think we're going to have to most fast on this, Craig. I spoke to the PM this morning and he said that as a last resort we are to offer a reward."

Craig gasped. "But that's not this country's policy!"

"No, that's right. We have to say it's being offered by friends and colleagues of Professor Hills."

"I see. Okay, I'll contact the press department."

"And what about the other thing I asked you to look into, Dr Wells?"

"I've got two people working on that now, sir. I can give you an update later on today."

"Right, that's good. Okay, well I'll speak to you later on – what time?"

"Five o'clock, if that's okay?"

"Just before that, if you wouldn't mind. I've got to update the PM at five."

"Certainly, sir.".

"And the reward news, that can be leaked straightaway, but not about finding the mobile phone, all right?"

"Yes, sir. I'll get onto that right away."

"Good work. Okay, speak to you later, Craig.

"Yes, will do. 'Bye."

Craig hung up and breathed a sigh of relief. Thank goodness he had just assigned two staff on Dr Wells. He was certainly going to take any information about him very seriously indeed.

A few hours later he had the results he was waiting for. The Professor had contacted Dr Wells four times over the last two weeks; once on the day he was abducted. But of more interest was the fact that Dr Wells had contacted the Romsey, Heath and Little Church Railway on six occasions before the Professor had gone missing.

CHAPTER ELEVEN
The Professor Awakes

WHEN the Professor fully came round it was midday. At first he was confused but then he saw Len staring at him, flung his blanket onto the floor and jumped up.

"What have you done to me!" he roared. "How dare you! Where have you taken me now?"

"Careful, Professor, you've got a chain round your leg."

The prisoner angrily tugged the chain attached to the pipe, then bent down and tried to remove it. Unfortunately, Derek had known what he was doing.

"I demand you release me! What right have you got to keep me here!"

"I'm sorry, Professor, truly I am. It's all got a bit silly now. But don't worry, we are going to release you."

"When?"

"Maybe tomorrow. We've just got to work something out."

"How to save your neck, you mean."

"The whole area is surrounded by armed guards. We don't want to get shot."

"Would serve you all right!" The Professor's eyes searched for his possessions. "And what the hell have you done to my briefcase?"

"Ah, well, it's on the table."

Despite their best efforts, he could see that it had been tampered with.

"You've opened it!"

"Sorry about that. But don't worry, I've got an old briefcase you can have upstairs."

The Professor threw himself back down onto the settee and put his head in his hands.

"I wish you hadn't done that. Now you're more at risk than I am."

"So as I was saying, we've just got to work something out. A plan. We don't want anything built here if it's going to interfere with the railway."

"You're sounding like a broken record. Do you think I could stop the government from doing anything, anyway?"

Len thought for a moment.

"Yes, I do. I think they'd listen to you. If you said this area wasn't suitable, for instance."

"Why should I do that?"

Just then a vibrating noise like thunder started overhead, getting closer and closer until the whole place shook. The Professor looked terrified.

"Don't worry, Mark, it's only one of our trains."

"My god, it sounds like it's right on top of us."

"It is, more or less."

The train made gave a loud, throaty whistle.

"Oh, that's the Thunderbolt. We should be hearing lots of different trains today, it's a gala day. I should be helping out, really."

"So sorry to be detaining you!" the Professor replied, sarcastically.

"Now, there's no need for that. I've said we're sorry. Well, I can see that you're upset so I'm going to go upstairs and give you some privacy. I'll come down in an hour or so with some lunch."

Len left the Professor to do the necessary and calm down a bit. He could see the man's point, he had a right to be angry. But Len still believed that he had the right to stick up for his beloved railway, too. He searched around for something for them both to eat. There were only a few tins of beans, soup and a packet of dried mash in the cupboard and some sausages, eggs and milk in the fridge. He checked the freezer compartment, revealing half a loaf of bread.

"Ye gods, I'm going to have to get some shopping!" he thought to himself. Len wondered about the ethics of leaving a tied up man in his cellar while he poodled off to buy some groceries. It didn't seem right, somehow. Not only that, it appeared that armed guards and sniffer dogs were searching the boot of everyone's car that drove past. They might catch the scent of the Professor on him. After some thought, Len decided the best option was to order a supermarket delivery. That's if the soldiers were letting them through, of course. He had never tried online shopping before, not being a big fan of the internet. But needs must, he thought to himself. It took him a good half an hour to finally order a £50 home delivery, and the earliest arrival was Sunday morning. They would have to scrape by until then.

Len looked at the kitchen clock. Only 20 minutes before the next train came past, and he wanted to be downstairs in time in case the Professor started panicking again. He remembered when the man had an asthma attack before; it had scared him almost as much as his victim. He hurriedly threw the remaining sausages on his grill and opened a few tins of beans. Better than nothing, he thought to himself.

To carry them downstairs would be a bit of a challenge. Len resolved this by covering each plate over with another and putting them on top of one another in a bucket. He then hurriedly boiled a kettle and filled a vacuum flask with tea and milk. He finished just as the whistle of an approaching train sounded in the distance.

Len opened the hatch and climbed back downstairs. He quickly scanned the gloom and was relieved to see the Professor standing up, watching him descend.

"Lunch is served!" he called out.

"I'm not hungry," came back the response.

"Come on, Professor, you must be hungry, you haven't eaten since yesterday afternoon."

"You might drug me again," he replied, tersely.

"No, I wouldn't do that, I promise." Len approached the Professor cautiously, and took the meals out of the bucket. "Look, you can pick which one you want to eat," he replied, as if to a reluctant child. "And the tea is in a flask, so if it's drugged we'll both be drinking it."

Len could feel the Professor weakening. "Oh, all right! I suppose I'd better keep my strength up."

"That's right," Len replied, soothingly. "It's a long walk to Downsend."

Just then the thunderous roar of another train passed overhead.

"Wait for the whistle – ah, there it is. Sounds like Delilah."

The Professor chewed a greasy sausage thoughtfully. "You mean you can tell which locomotive it is by the sound of its whistle?"

"More or less." Len warmed to his theme. "There's a couple of diesel engines so they sound completely different. And some of the trains are heavier than the others, so they vibrate more down here."

"Yes, what is this place, anyway?"

"Ahah, this is a left-over from the second world war. There's holes scattered all over the coastline, it's where they were going to pump oil to the troops under the sea to France."

"You mean this leads to a tunnel under the sea?"

"That's right." Len laughed. "Don't get too scared, they've all been blocked off now. Well, the ones they know about. I've kept the pump because I think it's interesting. I like engines."

"Hmm." The Professor was deep in thought. If he was going to build a bunker to store the country's nuclear waste he wanted it to be somewhere completely bullet proof; no hidden tunnels which might collapse and let the seawater in.

"I was wondering if you wanted any clean clothes to change into?"

"Thanks. But I wouldn't be able to change my trousers unless you took this chain off."

"Oh, right, I hadn't thought of that. I suppose I could give you a tee-shirt."

"Yes, and I suppose I should be grateful," the Professor replied sarcastically.

Len watched as the Professor ate his food hungrily. Then he poured two mugs of tea, wandered over to the bar area and rummaged around for some biscuits.

"Do you want the TV on?" he asked, managing to put some tea and biscuits near his captive without getting too close.

"Yes please, if you're going to insist on keeping me down here."

Len put the remote control by the Professor's tea and biscuits. They watched daytime television together in an awkward silence for a while until a loud whistle and the rumble of a train overhead interrupted them.

"That's Delilah on his way back from Downsend."

The Professor maintained a sulky silence, his empty plate and tea cup placed on a nearby table. Meanwhile, the midday news appeared on television.

"Police are offering a million pound reward for any information leading to the return of the missing scientist, Professor Hills," was the headline.

"Crikey, a million pounds!" Len spluttered.

They both watched in fascination. There were shots of police dogs combing the countryside and aerial views showing the area swarming with police and soldiers searching buildings.

"It's only a matter of time before they find me," the Professor remarked smugly.

Len stayed silent. He didn't want to upset the man by confessing that his property had already been searched. Then the camera zoomed in on a young man with a dark fringe and glasses.

"If anyone knows my father's whereabouts, please contact the police. He has bad asthma and needs his inhaler. Dad, if you are listening to this, please come home. We miss you..." his voice broke, *"You won't be in any trouble, just come home."*

As if to emphasise the point, the Professor grabbed his inhaler and took two puffs.

"Look what you've done!" he said croakily. "They think I've had some kind of nervous breakdown."

Len was at a loss what to say. He did feel guilty now he'd seen the Professor's son on TV, and could tell it had upset him.

"Well I'll just go back upstairs now, Mark, and see if I've had any messages."

He collected the plates and hurried back upstairs, leaving the man to grieve in private. No messages on his mobile phone from the others. Not surprising, really, because he knew they were all working today, except for Henry. He rang Henry's number.

"Trust him, never got his bloody phone on," he muttered, leaving a message asking him to call urgently.

Len then rummaged through his wardrobe in search of some clean clothing that the Professor could use. It might help to cheer him up, he thought. As he descended into the basement, Len heard the sound of metal grinding against metal before seeing the Professor jump back onto the settee.

"He's been trying to get loose," he thought to himself. But Len knew one thing for certain, if Derek had chained him up there was no way he was going to get loose, unless he cut his foot off. The thought did not please him; it was the sort of thing that desperate men did.

"I've brought some clothes down for you to wear, if you'd like," he called out, pretending he hadn't noticed anything.

"Okay, thanks," was the terse response.

Len walked over to the bar area and opened the cooler.

"I don't know about you, but I need a drink," he said, pulling open a can of beer and pouring it into a tankard. The Professor's eyes followed him. "Can I get you anything, Mark?" There was a pause.

"Do you have any cider?" he asked eventually.

"Of course, which type would you like?"

"Some *Magners*, if you have it."

"One pint of *Magners* coming up."

Len poured a can into one of his plastic glasses, just in case, before carefully putting it down beside his captive. After a few sips the ground started shaking again, and a steam locomotive passed overhead before blowing its whistle several times.

Len laughed. He knew that it was Derek in the driving seat, giving his usual 'hello' as he went past. It was reassuring to think they hadn't forgotten him.

"All right, what's the name of that one?" asked Mark, just for something to say.

"Okay, I'll give you a clue. One of our famous nurses."

"Florence Nightingale?"

"Correct! Well done, you can have another pint for that." Len opened the cooler, found another can of Magners and placed it carefully on the side table next to the Professor.

"You know I will need the toilet, especially if I drink this."

"No problem. Oh, I've got a camping toilet in the cupboard upstairs, why didn't I think of that?" Len went upstairs to find it, bringing down some toilet paper as well. When he came back he was surprised to see that the Professor was already pouring his second pint. "It might make my situation more bearable," he said when he noticed Len watching.

"Look Mark, as I've already said, we don't intend to keep you here much longer. We just need to all agree on what to do next."

Mark took another sip of cider. "If anything good has come out of this, I'm going to make more time for my family," he said thoughtfully. "I don't see my sons nearly enough. I've been so busy working on my project that it's taken over my life."

"I agree," said Len, taking a sip of bitter. "My wife didn't like me disappearing off to the railway all the time. I still don't think she should have left me just for that. It's not like I had an affair, like she did."

"My wife and I just drifted apart after the children left home," confessed the Professor. "I never dreamed she would leave me."

"Would you take her back?" Len asked keenly.

The Professor took another sip of cider and considered carefully.

"I don't know. I'd like to think we could give it another try. What about you?"

"No, I don't think I would," Len replied bitterly. "Not unless she begged me on bended knees," he mused, quite enjoying the thought. "And it would have to be on my terms. I want to be able to do what I like, when I like. If she doesn't like that, well…"

"Don't you miss having a woman around, though? Don't they make life a bit easier?"

"Not when they're nagging, they don't. I suppose they have their uses around the house, but that's about it."

"I bet she didn't like this place."

"Oh no, she never came down here. I only done it up after she left, just to spite her."

The Professor chuckled. "I suppose it is a bit of a hole."

"Agh, but there's good holes and bad holes." Len laughed. "And I'm not just talking about women here."

The Professor couldn't stop himself from laughing back, as the drink was starting to have an effect. "That's right. Dungeons, for example, they're bad holes."

"Well perhaps, but a man's shed, that's a good hole."

The Professor considered this, then added: "A hole in one, that's a good hole."

"A hole in your sock is a bad hole."

"Prison is a bad hole."

Len considered this. "Prison is a terrible hole. But at least my wife can't accuse me of being boring."

The Professor laughed then, and they had a good laugh together.

"Seriously," gasped Mark, "You do need to get a life, and so do I. I tell you what, when you get out of prison, I'll take you for a round of golf."

"Great, I've never played before and there's some good courses round here. Don't suppose I'd get a hole in one, though."

"You might be good at it."

"Okay, deal."

"Len, I'd like a bit of privacy now, if you wouldn't mind."

"Oh right, I get it. Okay, I'll go back upstairs, and I won't come down until tea-time. Unless you want something, of course. Just bang on these pipes and I'll hear it."

"Okay, thanks."

Len went back to his kitchen and left Mark to his own devices. "I think that went quite well, considering," he smiled to himself. Now, if only Henry would pick up his phone and give his agreement to letting Mark loose on Monday, they could start making arrangements. He tried again, with no luck.

CHAPTER TWELVE
Henry's Story

HENRY was the oldest of the group; at 73 he could remember when real steam trains ran on the tracks at the back of his home in Clapham Junction. When he was a small boy his mother would stand him at the window and he would wave at the drivers as they went past, and they got to know him and many would hoot their horns as they went by. To this day he still got a shiver of excitement when he heard the steam trains sounding their hooters on the miniature railway.

When he reached 17 there was only thing that Henry wanted to do; be a train driver. And finally, after working his way up from guard, fireman and assistant driver he had finally became the driver of a steam engine. But times changed and they were on the wane, with new diesel locomotives taking over in the 1960s. He had more than once driven a steam engine on its final voyage to the scrap yard. These journeys were always full of other train drivers travelling on the engine, paying their last respects on its final ride. The diesel locomotives made for a poor substitute, in his view.

So it was not very surprising to anyone who knew Henry that on retiring from the national railways he had headed straight for the nearest working steam railway and offered his services. Since 2005 he had spent almost every day helping out at the RHLR. It had helped him get over the loss of his beloved wife, Minty, and the fact that his two sons had both emigrated; one to Australia and the other to New Zealand. The railway and the friends he had made there were a real lifeline.

"I'm not just going to stand by and watch any more steam locomotives go the scrapyard," he thought to himself.

Henry did have a second love, however – Bowls. He was captain of the Romsey Sands Bowls Club first team, and met regularly with his team mates to play matches against other clubs. This fact had been noted by the forensic data analysis team who had spotted regular outgoing from his bank account to the Club and then found that he was also the Treasurer of the Bowls Club bank account. Henry's priority this Saturday was the end of season tournament with one of their biggest rivals, Heath & District, hence he was unable to work at the railway until Sunday.

Blissfully unaware of the attention being foisted on him, and with his mobile phone switched off as usual, Henry arrived at the Club early to meet two potential members who had rung earlier in the week. Agents 41 and 42, who had been assigned to follow Henry, were caught unawares when he spotted them sitting in their car outside the Club, and walked over to them.

"Hello, you must be John and Terry," he'd said.

One said 'yes' and the other, 'no'. Henry laughed.

"You don't sound too sure. Come on, lads, there's nothing to be ashamed about playing bowls any more, it's a young man's game now. Let me show you around."

The agents both looked at each other, got out of their car and followed him.

"You must be Henry," said Agent 41, thinking on his feet. "Yes, we'd love to see everything before we decide whether to join or not."

Henry led them into the pavilion to a small room on the left-hand side. The walls were lined with full length metal lockers.

"This is the gent's changing room. When you join you get your own locker to keep your bowling gear in. Now then, would you gents like a roll up?"

The two men looked at each other, registering their shock. Henry saw this and after a few moments laughed.

"Ha ha, I can see you've got the wrong idea. Oh dear!" He chuckled to himself. "That's what we call a game of bowls. I'll need to get you both some shoes to wear on the green. What size are you, John?"

"Size 10, me."

"And you? Sorry, what's your name?"

No 42 smiled. "Yes, sorry, I am Terry. I'm a size 11."

"Okay then. Judging by that, I'll get John a size 7 and you a size 8 set of bowls. Usually feet and hand sizes go together. I'll be back in a minute."

While Henry wandered off to search for spare bowls and shoes, the men looked at each other and laughed.

"Do you think our man could be hidden in one of these lockers?" Agent 41 scanned the room carefully.

"It's possible," said the other. They went round the room trying to peer through the ventilation holes in the top, at the same time listening for Henry to return.

"What do we do if John and Terry turn up?"

"We'll worry about that when it happens. At least this gives us a chance to check the place out."

After a few minutes, Henry came back carrying two sets of shoes in one hand and two sets of bowls in string bags in the other. The men took them off him as they could see he was struggling a bit.

"You know what they say about stepping into dead man's shoes," Henry chuckled. "No, just ignore me, there's nothing wrong with them."

Agents 41 and 42 reluctantly put them on, giving each other knowing looks.

"Do they fit all right? Good. Come on then, before the tournament starts."

The men followed obediently.

"I must say you are both looking very smart. That's one thing we're strict on, the men all have to wear a blazer and a hat on Club nights. Come on then, you can step onto the green now. You see this small white ball, that's the jack. I'm going to roll it three-quarters of the way down the green. Well, try to; now you're watching it will probably go into the ditch."

Henry rolled the jack expertly up the green.

"Now, we'll start with you, John. Pick the first bowl up. You can see it's got a small circle and a big circle on it. They don't roll perfectly straight, they always turn in towards the bias, the small circle. So whether you want to reach the jack on the right or the left hand side you always have the small circle facing inwards. Okay, stand on the mat and give it a try."

There followed an enjoyable half-hour of lawn bowls, with the men getting more competitive with every roll. Henry told them they were both very good and would love to have them join the Club.

"Oh yes, I'd love to see the rest of the Club house," said Terry enthusiastically.

"Can we have a list of fixtures?" asked John.

Henry obliged them and showed them round the rest of the pavilion, all except for the female changing room.

"Even I don't get to go in there," he joked.

The agents removed the bowls shoes and got ready to leave.

"Well, thank you very much for your time, sir."

"Oh, no problem at all," Henry beamed, enjoying being called 'sir'.

The men both shook hands with him and left.

"What do we do now we've blown our cover?" asked Agent 42.

"We'll have to make an urgent request for backup," Agent 41 replied. "But seriously, I don't suspect him for one minute, do you?"

"You know what they taught us, never to trust anybody. But no, I have to agree, I don't think he's got anything to do with the Professor's disappearance. I think he didn't get a proper look at the suspects and has just used his imagination to describe them."

"Who's going to be the bearer of bad news?" asked Agent 41. They tossed a coin.

"Heads! Oh no!" The job of relaying this information to Craig had fallen to Agent 42.

Later, a confused Henry picked up a message on his mobile phone from John apologising for not being able to make it that day. He recounted the story after the tournament to his colleagues on the veranda.

"You really must stop approaching strange men in car parks," joked Arthur.

Henry flushed as the ladies on the next table giggled. He had a soft spot for Phyllis, seated nearby, and he didn't want her to get the wrong idea about him.

Meanwhile, as Henry was busy at his Bowls club, his house was being expertly searched from top to bottom, with nothing untoward found.

On the way home he stopped at the Lotus House and picked up his Chinese takeaway, which he was in the habit of doing at the weekends. When he arrived indoors he saw the answerphone flashing, and listened to several desperate sounding messages from Len asking him to come round on Sunday after work. Henry had been so busy he had almost managed to forget about the kidnapped Professor stashed away in Len's basement. He would have to catch up with the boys on Sunday about what happened after he had left them and driven back to the station on the Baron Hughie.

CHAPTER THIRTEEN
Positive ID

DCI WILLIS received an urgent phone call on his newly installed landline just after 6.00pm on Saturday.

"Sir, it's Janice. I can't get hold of DS Dunwoody, his line is permanently engaged." She sounded breathless, as if she had been hurrying.

"Don't worry, you can always call me as well. What's up?"

"We're at the home of the Thompson's, the family in the first carriage of the train. Although they didn't see very much of the incident, one of the young boys, Alex, has identified somebody from the railway staff photograph as being the farmer."

"Excellent! What do his mother and father say?"

"Yes, they've had a look at it too and on reflection, they say he does look very similar."

"That's very encouraging, well done. Do we know the name of this particular person?"

"Not yet, sir – it's just a group photograph from the last Christmas party."

"I see. Can you hot foot it back to the railway and ask the Station Master to identify this person?"

"Yes, sir. I'm not sure whether it's still open though."

"Right, give them a ring and ask for Mr Cuthbert – that's the Station Master – and if he'd mind waiting until you get there, would you?"

"Yes, will do that right now."

"You don't know who was interviewing the other family, do you?"

"I think it's Sergeants Dean and Walters, sir."

"Right, hopefully they are still with them or else I'll have to send them back. All right, Janice, I'll leave you to deal with the Station Master and I'll get on to those two. Give me a catch up later on, won't you?"

"Yes, sir, as soon as I've spoken to him."

"Thanks, 'bye then."

Willis hurriedly searched through his phone list and found Dean's number first.

"Hello, Sergeant Dean?"

"Yes, who's this please?"

"Phil, it's me, DCI Willis. I believe you were interviewing some of the witnesses on the train?"

"Yes, sir, we've just spoken to Irene Tremayne. We've shown her the photograph and she thinks, but she's not sure, that she recognises two of the men as the ones who got onto the train after the Professor."

"Oh! You've all got the same photograph, I take it?"

"Yes, sir, it's a group photograph."

"So whereabouts on the photo are the two possible suspects?"

"On the left hand side, sir, standing next to each other."

"Well, somehow that makes it more interesting. Did she recognise the farmer at all?"

"No sir."

"Sorry to be a pain, but can you go back to her and ask if she'd come along to the railway tomorrow and do an identification?"

"Right, will do."

"What about the other two that were with her? Have you spoken to them?"

"That's Sergeant Walters, sir."

"All right. Can you liaise with him and ask them to come along as well, and let me know?"

"Yes sir."

"Good work, Sergeant. I'll contact the railway and ask for their staff identification details, so don't worry about that.

If you just arrange the pick up tomorrow with DS Dunwoody, okay?"

"Yes sir, will do."

As soon as he hung up he dialled the number for the railway and got through to Mr Cuthbert, the station master. There followed a brief conversation where he confirmed that a female police officer was on her way and he was waiting for her to arrive. Willis updated him on the additional suspects that needed identification, and requested their personal details and addresses to be given to Janice urgently, as well as all the others in the photograph. Then Willis wandered off to find Woody, who was still speaking on his mobile when he found him. "

"Hang on a minute," he said to the caller. "Sir, I've got the Met on the phone and they've found the Professor's mobile."

"Wonderful! Still no sign of the Professor, then?"

"No, nothing at all. But the phone's already been rushed here for prints and analysis."

"And whereabouts was it, after all?"

"What was the name of the field? Oh yes, Monty's field, nearby to where the train stopped."

"Great! Okay, Woody, I'll let you finish your call. Then I've got some news to tell you, too. I'll be in my room," he said, before wandering back to his shared office cum stationery cupboard. A few minutes later, DS Dunwoody joined him.

"I take it our friend Craig knows about the phone, then?"

"He must do, sir, they found it about 11 o'clock."

"And he didn't think to let us know? That's not very team-spirited, is it?" said Willis, frowning. "Hmm. Well I'm half tempted not to update him with our news but that would be extremely petty, don't you think?"

Woody laughed, then looked puzzled. "What is our news, sir?"

"The witnesses have only gone and identified three of the suspects from the railway photograph."

"Really! Are we going to arrest them?"

"Not yet, hold your horses. That's why I'm considering not telling Craig. We've got to take the softly, softly approach here. Imagine, they've got the Professor holed up somewhere since Friday morning. They've got to keep him fed and watered, obviously, and I shouldn't think they want to get caught, either. If we bring them all in for questioning, who's going to be looking after the Professor?"

"Good point."

"And we don't want them panicking if they think we suspect them, and just leaving the man to his fate."

"No, we might never find him then."

"Quite. So what I've arranged is for Janice and the team to escort the witnesses to the railway tomorrow to see if they can give a proper identification seeing them all in the flesh."

"Great idea. And then having them followed?"

"Yes, now we agree on something. So we'll need to ask Craig for help with that, anyway."

"What about the man he's already having followed?"

"The ticket inspector; Henry, wasn't it? We'll ask Craig how that's going as well." Willis rose out of his seat and they both went off to find him.

CHAPTER FOURTEEN
The Net Tightens

THE two men walked into HQ to find Craig having a sandwich and a mug of coffee.

"No, it's okay, don't get up," said Willis, in case Craig was going to.

"Oh hello, Simon," Craig replied, looking embarrassed. "I've been meaning to speak to you this afternoon, but it's been non-stop."

"So I hear," Willis replied, somewhat sarcastically. "Shall I come back when you've finished?"

Craig took a sip from his coffee and then indicated the two men should sit down. "No, it would be good to have a catch up. How is your investigation going?"

Willis and Woody pulled a chair up beside his desk and sat down.

"Rather well, actually. In fact, now that you've found the Professor's telephone, I wondered if you'd had a chance to check it for prints?"

"How did you – oh, I see – yes, I meant to tell you this afternoon, but we've been doing forensics on his telephone account and trying to trace all his phone calls. Apart from the fingerprinting, of course. Nothing interesting to note there, unfortunately. We have found out something, though."

"Yes? I'm all ears." Willis leaned forward.

"It all seems to be coming back to the same question; how did anybody know that the Professor was going to be on that particular train sitting in that compartment at that particular time?"

"Yes, we've been pondering the same question."

"We've been looking at Dr Wells' telephone calls, and it appears that he contacted the Railway on at least six occasions in the weeks leading up to the Professor's disappearance."

"Really?" Willis looked at Woody. "That *is* interesting. It ties in very nicely with our investigations."

Now it was Craig's turn to look interested. "Have you found something out about Dr Wells?"

"Not Dr Wells, no. He's not been on our remit. But we have had the witnesses look at a photograph of the railway staff taken last Christmas, and three of the suspects have potentially been identified."

"Really?" Craig leapt out of his chair. "Do we have their names and addresses?"

Willis indicated that Craig should sit back down.

"We're not rushing into this because it is only a photograph, and not a particularly good one at that. So we're bringing the witnesses in to the Railway Station tomorrow to have a look at the staff in person."

"That's a good idea, but what if the men don't show up?"

"They're all due to work on Sunday, we've checked," said Woody.

"In answer to your question, yes, we have identified the potential suspects involved, and are getting their names and addresses," continued Willis. "We want your help again to have these people followed."

"Yes, no problem at all. Just to update you on that, we have been tailing the Guard, Henry Smith, all day today."

"Oh yes, I meant to ask you how that went," Willis replied.

"Well, nothing to report as yet. He attended a bowling match all day, got a takeaway and then went home. We did have his house searched, however, while he was out."

"Good. Find anything?"

"Nothing at all. We even checked in the Chinese takeaway on how much food he ordered, but it was his usual takeaway meal for one."

"But in light of what we've discovered today, I think we should continue watching him, if that's possible?"

"Yes, of course. If you provide me with the names and addresses of the others you'd like watched, I'll get straight onto it."

"Thanks. We're just waiting for confirmation. Right, if there's nothing else we can leave you in peace." Willis got up to leave. "But you will keep us informed of any developments, won't you?"

There was a short silence.

"Yes, of course," Craig replied, before the men left.

After they'd left, Craig gave a sigh of relief. Thank goodness that Mason had insisted earlier that he continue to get Henry Smith followed. Agents 41 and 42 had convinced him that it was a waste of time. It did now sound as if this plot was a conspiracy, with Dr Wells as the ringleader. He picked up the telephone and spoke to the Aerial Support Unit. He wanted heat-seeking cameras to pass over Dr Wells' house and check on the property. They had already ascertained that he lived there with his wife and three children, according to the council tax register. On Craig's map the place looked like a large farmhouse with several outbuildings.

Craig wandered over to where Geoff was still working on Dr Wells' mobile phone calls.

"Anything interesting yet?" he asked.

"Yes, sir, we have managed to establish that he sent a text message last Sunday at 1pm from the vicinity of Romsey Station to another mobile also in the same location."

"Good work! Who was the message sent to?"

"I'm afraid it's an old pay-as-you-go mobile phone which is unregistered and has no satellite detection."

"Blast! Keep trying to trace the recipient, won't you. What did the message say?"

Geoff showed him the print-out. Half an hour later Craig was waiting anxiously for the update from the helicopter search so that he could either go back to his hotel or make other plans. Finally, the news came.

"Mr Bennett? John Baldwin, Captain here." The noise of the chopper almost drowned out the speaker, who was shouting into his earpiece.

"Yes, go ahead."

"It's quite a large property with what looks like outbuildings on the left hand side."

"Did you find any heat sources?"

"Yes, there appear to be five heat sources in the main building and another in one of the outbuildings."

"I see. Can you tell what these sources are? Is it a fire, for example?"

"No, the heat shapes resemble persons. The heat from radiators gives off a different kind of shape."

"Okay. Can you see the shapes moving around?"

"Not the one in the outbuilding, but the ones in the main building, yes."

"Thanks very much, Mr Baldwin, that's the information I require."

"Do you want us to keep hovering over the property?"

Craig thought quickly. "No, I don't think we want to alert the householders to anything. That will do for now, thanks."

"Okay, sir, we'll return to base. Over and out."

Craig paced the room excitedly. He considered contacting Peter Mason, but thought better of it. He had spoken to him less than an hour ago, and Peter had already said that he was taking his daughter out for the evening. Here was his chance to show that he could handle the job and capture the Professor before PC Plod got there first. He called his evening team together and made plans for a dawn raid.

CHAPTER FIFTEEN
Saturday Night

IT HAD been a busy and successful day at the RHLR with over 600 visitors. Station Master George Cuthbert was in the process of tidying up the shop and closing everything down ready for Sunday, when the phone call came. Now he was facing a terrible dilemma. He could not believe that he was having to give out personal details of some of his most trusted and long-serving members of staff to the police. To make things worse, they were all down for volunteer duty on Sunday. It sounded as if they would be walking into a trap and were going to get arrested. He felt as if he should call them and warn them all not to show up.

George thought carefully back to the day of the incident. It had been a perfectly normal afternoon, no different from any other Friday. Henry had been on duty, so he had not been there at the time. The whole thing just didn't make sense, and he could not accept that any of his staff had been involved in the kidnapping. True, there had been mutterings in the canteen about the nuclear dump site and fears that they would dig up the railway track. If his men had been involved in any way at all it was out of love for the railway, and now he was being asked to dob them in.

George looked at the original copy of the Christmas photograph. They'd had such a good time last year after the Santa's Grotto trip. He looked at the photos of Roy and Alan, standing together as usual, with Derek, Henry and Len not too far away.

"As thick as thieves," he thought to himself, then gave a nervous laugh. If they had 'stolen' the Professor, they really were thick.

Another thought puzzled him, they had not asked for details about Len, even though he had been driving the train at the time. George checked his records for the umpteenth time. Yes, there he was, driving the Green Dawn. *Green Dawn* – the thought suddenly struck him, how ironic! He paused to listen to the news on the radio.

"*A million pounds reward has been offered for any information leading to the discovery of Professor Hills.*"

George grabbed the side of the counter to steady himself. If any of his boys were responsible, as he was beginning to suspect they might be, they were in big trouble! His thoughts wandered back to Len. Len was just as close to Alan, Roy, Henry and Derek as anyone. If Len was driving the train when the Professor was kidnapped by the others he would also have been involved, no two ways about it. But what could they possibly have done with him? He gasped out loud as he remembered something – Len's Den. No, that wasn't right. He thought carefully. Len's shed, that was it! A great big bloody hole in the ground in his back garden, which he'd made into a basement. A perfect hiding place to put someone who was kidnapped!

Thoughts of the million pound reward surfaced in his mind. No, he would not do it, betray his friends for a million quid or any other amount of money. They were doing it to save the railway, and he would support them as much as he could without saying anything to anyone. He just hoped that they weren't going to do anything stupid. How many others knew about Len's shed, he thought to himself? Just a few others, maybe, and of course Roy and Alan's wives, because the boys were always escaping to it.

A short while later, two police officers turned up in a car outside. He quickly printed off the contact details he had for all his staff and studied it. He wasn't going to give them this. He would only give the address and landline numbers for the men they asked for, but not their mobile phone details. He suspected, if anything, the lads would be communicating with each other that way. No point in speeding up the inevitable. He faked a smile for the female officer as she entered the shop.

"Hello, I've kept the place open for you."

The officers approached and flashed their IDs.

"Hello, you must be Mr Cuthbert?" asked Janice.

"That's right, I spoke to you on the phone."

"Hello sir, I'm PC Goldsmith and this is my colleague, PC Stayton."

"Yes, hello both of you."

"Good afternoon." PC Howard Stayton introduced himself.

"Mr Cuthbert, as I explained earlier, we are here to collect the names and addresses of some members of your staff in this photo you kindly gave us earlier. Do you have them for me now, please?" Janice asked.

George looked at the photograph she was holding.

"Which ones in particular?"

"We want the details of all your staff members," Stayton replied.

"All of them?"

"Yes please, not just the ones in the photo. Do you have them to hand?"

George looked at the female officer.

"My colleague is correct, we do need all the names of members of staff, but in particular, these three on the photograph." She indicated to Roy, Alan and Derek.

George sighed and handed over the printout he had just run off the computer. "Here's the list of everybody's name and address. You will see Derek's name here, and Roy and Alan further down."

"What are their surnames?" asked the male officer, opening his notebook.

"Derek Barton, Roy King and Alan Rochester."

"Thank you."

Janice scanned the printout. "You wouldn't have their mobile numbers, would you?"

"No, I'm afraid not."

"I see. Well thanks very much. And will those people be here tomorrow?"

"Yes, should be. They're on duty."

"Okay, that's great."

"What about the other men who were here the day the Professor was kidnapped?" asked Stayton, searching through his notebook. "A Mr Len Sutton and a Mr Henry Smith?"

"Yes, Henry should be back tomorrow. I doubt if Len will be here, though, he's off sick."

PC Stayton scribbled something in his notebook. "Do you know what's wrong with him?" he asked.

"No I don't. Look, these people are all volunteers, they're not obliged to come here at all."

"No, we realise that, Mr Cuthbert," said Janice soothingly. "Well that's everything for now, thank you very much. We will be back again tomorrow, but thanks for your help."

"Okay, thank you."

Mr Cuthbert let them both out of the shop and bolted the door. When he saw them drive off he heaved a sigh of relief. Phew! They hadn't seemed too suspicious when he'd told them Len was off sick. Because it sounded very suspicious to him. Len had never taken a day off sick in all the years he had known him.

CHAPTER SIXTEEN
Pavlov's Dog

LEN had discreetly left his captive on his own for four hours on Saturday afternoon. In the main, because he was hoping that one of his friends, in particular Henry, would contact him and help him decide what to do with the Professor next. It was all very well for him just to let the man loose, but what if he turned nasty? He wanted Derek to be there, at least, to make sure that all went well. They also needed to decide on timing and method. For instance, the middle of the night in the back of the coal truck being his preferred time and method, but with the armed guard on full alert, even this seemed fraught with danger. These four hours had given him time to think, which was not possible to do when staring at his victim.

Now there was the problem of what to cook for tea. It would have to be scrambled egg and beans on toast, which wasn't a lot for a grown man to eat all evening. But then, he reasoned, Mark hadn't done a lot of exercise being tied up to a pipe all day. The whole thing was beginning to get on his nerves and he wanted to get rid of this man as soon as possible. Len accepted that they were all going to get caught and no doubt he would be going to prison, but was quite happy to accept the blame as it had been his idea to start with. He would just say that the others went along with him because he'd asked them to.

Len set about half-heartedly rustling up the remnants of his fridge into a meal for two. It was times like this that he missed Alice, busying herself in the kitchen. He was sure she would have thought of something far more inventive with the same ingredients. Len took extra care not to burn the last few eggs in his saucepan, throwing in plenty of milk and marge and stirring all the time. Then he sprinkled on some salt and pepper and tasted the result. Not bad! If the professor left any, he'd eat it himself. The beans were ready at the same time as the toast popped out of the toaster, nicely done.

In the distance Len could hear the hoot from a steam train approaching, so he quickly made another flask of tea and repeated the morning's procedure, putting upturned plates on top of each other inside a bucket, before carefully opening the hatch and making his way back downstairs. By this time the train had reached Romsey Sands, and blew its horn as it thundered overhead.

Len noticed that the Professor seemed agitated, pacing back and forth as far as the chain would let him.

"No! Ugh! I can't believe it, I'm salivating!" He sounded disgusted about something.

"Sorry, what's wrong, is it my cooking?" Len asked, startled to see this change in him.

"It's your fault! Always bringing food down when the train goes past, when it sounds the horn. You've turned me into an animal! Now every time I hear the train whistle I start salivating, just like Pavlov's dog!"

"Like what? Sorry, you've lost me."

"Pavlov's dog! Pavlov was a scientist who used to play a metronome every time he fed his dog. In the end the dog salivated every time it heard the ticking, whether he fed it or not. And that's what you've done to me!" The Professor threw himself down onto the sofa, threw his head in his hands and started weeping.

Len watched him, feeling sorry for causing such distress.

"Sorry about that, I didn't mean to do it. Is it permanent?"

The Professor continued to sob into his hands, looking totally bereft.

"Probably! When I heard the first signal, my mouth started watering. Then as I heard the train get closer it got worse. By the time you opened the hatch I was positively drooling. I'm turning into an animal! You can't keep me like this!"

Len felt incredibly guilty.

"I'm sorry, I won't do it again."

The Professor continued to sob.

"Look, Mark, I've already decided that whatever happens, I'm going to let you go."

Mark quietened down and looked up at him.

"When, now? Please?"

Len sat down on a bar stool.

"Tomorrow – Sunday – I'll ask the others to come round here after work and we'll arrange to get you back to Downsend."

"What if they say no?"

Len paused and thought about it. "If they say no, I'll let you go on Monday, after they've left. I'll tell them you've escaped."

"Really?" The Professor brightened up. "I'll try to stick up for you, tell them you looked after me." He paused. "I can't promise to do the same for that thug who attacked me."

"Derek? Oh, I didn't mean to say that. Well, I suppose you would have found out his name, anyway."

The Professor remained silent.

"Derek's a great guy, but he's damaged. He was a soldier in Bosnia and saw some terrible things over there. He wasn't the same person when he came back. The railway's been great for helping him get over his post-traumatic stress. At first, whenever the trains used to blow their whistle he used to jump a mile in the air. Now he's trigger happy on them."

"Aah, I see." Mark thought back to hearing Len laugh when one of the trains passed overhead. "That's Derek who makes that horrible racket when he goes past, isn't it?"

"Ha ha, you've sussed it. You see, he's not so scary when you think about it, is he?"

"No, I suppose not."

Seeing that the Professor had cheered up a little, Len took the opportunity to unload the plated food from his bucket and place it on a nearby table, together with the flask.

"I'll leave these here, you might decide you want them later on."

With that, he discreetly made for the camper loo and carried that and his own bucket of food back up the stairs. Then he made a final decision. Enough was enough! If the others hadn't contacted him by tomorrow he was letting the man go free. It was obvious that Mark couldn't take being chained up like an animal for much longer. Rifling through his address book he rang all of the gang's mobile numbers asking them to call round on Sunday evening to make plans for Mark's release.

Len's own stomach was rumbling as he sat down to eat his tea. He prayed that nothing would go wrong with his Sunday morning home delivery, especially if the Professor was getting hungry every time a train went past.

CHAPTER SEVENTEEN
Derek's chase

ONE of the advantages of volunteering for the railway was that you got reduced travel on the trains. This was quite handy for Derek as he was currently banned from driving after a particularly unpleasant incident in New Romsey when he'd had an altercation with a taxi driver. In reality the journey was usually free, depending on who was driving the train. This meant that most Sunday mornings he would catch the train and head to Heath to get his shopping in the cut-price supermarket, Dial, at the end of the line. Then he would have a chat with his mates back at Heath depot before catching the train home complete with his bags of shopping.

Today was a little different because he was due to start work at one o'clock at the *Vintage Weekend*, which meant he didn't have much time to get washed and dressed and up to Heath and back before arriving at New Romsey ready for work. He had received Len's message that they were all meeting up in his shed afterwards.

Getting up early was not a problem for Derek. The army training had instilled in him a strict routine and every day he would leap out of bed, hangover or not, at 6am and get washed, shaved and dressed. Then he liked to go for a run round the block, but this morning he was too busy getting his vintage costume pressed for later and then polishing his boots. He put on the radio and was whistling tunelessly when he heard the news of the one million pound reward. Derek gave a long drawn out whistle and stopped shining his boots to listen properly. He'd thought those nuclear diagrams were worth something, and now he was proven right! They would definitely have to discuss this when they met up later.

Derek arrived at New Romsey ready for the first departure to Heath at 9.35 which would arrive at 10.10. The cut-price supermarket opened at 10 o'clock so he could just walk straight in, get his bits and pieces and catch the 11.15 heading back to New Romsey. That would arrive back at 11.50, giving him just over an hour to have some dinner, shower and dress, ready for work. That was what he loved about the railway, the routine. It made him feel safe.

"All right, Andy?" Derek called out to his train driver, who was aboard 'Adonis'.

"Yeah great, are you in later?"

"Just getting some shopping, then I'm back for one o'clock. I'm driving Delilah and Dark Prince."

"You'd better check, I think Dark Prince has blown a gasket."

"Oh right, cheers. Did you hear about the million pound reward for that Professor?"

Andy laughed. "If I'd known he was that valuable I'd have took him myself."

Derek laughed hesitantly, not sure if Andy knew more than he was letting on. "Have they still got police at all the stations?"

"Worse than yesterday, the place is crawling with them."

Derek looked around and spotted a police car in the car park. "Right, well I'd better get on the train, you should be off in a minute."

Normally Derek would have offered to stand next to the driver of the engine just for company, but he decided to keep his head down, literally, and got inside a miniature carriage instead. It was amazing to see the train already full, especially at this time of year when sometimes they ran empty. It was a good thing they organised these special events to help keep the railway going.

"Thank goodness they never cancelled it," he thought to himself, having heard it was a close-run thing.

Derek climbed out at Heath Station to see banners flying and the car park full of vintage cars and buses, the same as the day before. He headed over to the white Rolls and spoke to Jenny, who was dressed up beautifully as Mary Poppins.

"Hello gorgeous," he winked at her. She extended a white-gloved hand and he kissed it. "Can I give you a ride later?"

Jenny chuckled and Derek laughed back. A bit of harmless flirting never hurt, he thought to himself. Shame she was already married. Suddenly the hairs on the back of his neck bristled and he stopped dead. He had learnt never to ignore his instincts, which told him that someone was watching him. He turned round and saw two men, dressed like off-duty Mormons, staring at him from the other side of the platform. When they saw him looking at them they turned away. Derek weighed them up quickly. They didn't look like the usual train spotter type. A bit too young for one thing and for another, no cameras hanging round their necks. They could just be looking at Jenny, pretty as she was, but Derek thought it best to make a move.

"I'd better be off," he said to her, winking again. "See you later."

"Okay 'bye darling," she replied.

In a few swift strides he had left the station, darted across the main road and entered the park beside the Military Canal.

This route was a pleasant short cut through to Dial's Supermarket. Derek practised his 'fast slow walk'. He had learnt this as a kid, as well as the 'slow fast walk'. It involved keeping the top half of his body very still but lengthening his stride at the same time. The effect made it appear as if he was just strolling along, when actually he was moving faster than a slow jog. After fifty yards he turned and looked back over his shoulder. Yes, they were still there! Again, army survival training came to the fore. He kept walking as if going in a straight line and then suddenly darted to the left, running over a small wooden bridge that led over the canal to the main road. When he reached the other side he dived behind a large bush and crouched down, watching to see if the men also crossed the bridge.

A few seconds later he saw one of the men running across the bridge and looking both ways. The other man had not been able to run as fast but would no doubt soon be following. Derek knew he had to act quickly. He grabbed the man round his ankles and yanked hard, pulling the man to the ground and then delivering his famous knock-out punch. This worked immediately and he dragged him into the bushes beside him. The next man followed about thirty seconds later. He looked around bewildered trying to find where his colleague, and Derek, had disappeared to. As soon as he got close enough, Derek pulled the same trick and had them both out cold in the bushes beside the river. Without stopping to think he searched their pockets and found their mobile phones, which he tossed into the river. With a small sigh he threw in his own. Then he sprinted off as fast as he could back into the park and hired a small rowing boat, from which he rowed as fast as possible away from the scene.

Years ago Derek had trained as a solider at Heath camp and he knew the area well. At the other end of the canal he went ashore and caught the first bus to Folkestone, considering all the while what to do next. He would have to change his appearance he realised; also, he had to draw £500 out of a cashpoint as soon as possible before his bank account was blocked, and then get as far away from there as he could. After drawing out the cash he went into the nearest charity shop and bought some clothes and an old rucksack, then entered a Chemist shop and bought some clippers and a pair of sunglasses. Next, he went into the bus station toilets, shaved his head and changed into the new clothes, putting the old ones into his rucksack. Finally, he put on the pair of sunglasses.

"I look better than normal," he thought to himself, smiling at his cool new image.

Derek had one plan in mind, and that was to get to north Wales at the earliest opportunity, by nightfall if possible. He knew the area around the Brecon Beacons very well having spent time training there, and thought he would be able to survive a while provided he purchased a tent and some camping equipment. Then, when all the fuss had died down and the Professor had been discovered, he would look around for a job in a pub somewhere and start his life again. There was even a steam railway on Mount Snowdon, he remembered; perhaps he could get some work there.

Decision made, he headed for Folkestone Central and caught the first high speed train to London.

CHAPTER EIGHTEEN
George to the Rescue

LEN was up bright and early on Sunday, ready for his morning delivery of groceries which was due between 8.00 and 9.00am. He used up the last of the bread and made some toast and a flask of tea, before heading down into the cellar to check on his prisoner. It looked like Mark was still asleep, so he crept in and quietly placed the breakfast close by before creeping back upstairs again. He looked cautiously outside and noted that the army still appeared to be patrolling The Parade and the beach opposite him.

Len jumped when the doorbell rang. Peering through the spyhole, he spotted The Saints delivery van outside. With relief, he threw open the front door.

"Ten bags of shopping for you, sir?"

"Yes, that's right."

The driver unloaded the bags from his crates and carried them to the front door.

"I'm surprised they let you through, it's like Fort Knox out there," Len joked.

"I was surprised they never stopped me, too," he replied.

Len signed for his bags and carried them inside before quickly shutting the front door. He had just finished putting the groceries away when his doorbell rang again. His heart pounding, he carefully peered through his spyhole again. Len gave a sigh of relief. It was only Ryan, the newspaper lad. Every week Ryan would knock on the door in the pretence that he couldn't get the newspaper through his letterbox, and every week Len would hand over a £1 coin as a tip.

"Hello Ryan, I'm pleased to see you," he replied, giving him a smile.

"Here's your paper," Ryan said as normal.

Len went for his wallet and handed over a pound coin, as usual.

"Thanks very much. Er, Mr Sutton?" Ryan hesitated.

"Yes?"

Ryan shuffled, looking embarrassed. "Did you just have a home delivery?"

"Yes. Why, is everything all right?"

"Well, I was cycling up the road on my bike and I saw the man deliver your shopping." He lowered his voice and stood closer. "And then I saw two men parked in a car over the road – no, don't look!" he hissed. "Anyway, the thing is, those men went and spoke to the driver and they gave him some money – I couldn't see how much – and it looked like he gave them the receipts for your shopping."

"Really?" Len was suddenly terrified, summoning all his strength not to peer at the offending vehicle. "Well, thanks very much, Ryan. Thank you for telling me!"

"That's okay," he replied, turning to leave. "Hope everything's all right," he mumbled, before climbing onto his bike and riding off.

Len shut the door firmly behind him, breathing heavily. Placing the newspaper on the kitchen worktop he crept up his chalet extension staircase and knelt down on the floor by the window, peering as invisibly at he could through the net curtains.

"Damn!" Ryan was right, there was a car opposite his house with two men inside. He could even see them reading what appeared to be his shopping list. What was that Mark had said? *"Now you're more at risk than I am."*

"I've got to get the Professor out of here as soon as possible, if I don't want to get caught," he thought again.

Len searched under his bed until he found his old briefcase, pulled it out and rubbed the dust off the top. Time to get rid of Mark, and his nuclear plans, as quickly as possible. He rushed back down to the kitchen, put the briefcase on the floor and unpacked his shopping. There did seem to be an inordinate amount of ready meals for somebody living alone. In fact, all round it did look very suspicious, he decided. He made a pot of tea and poured himself a mug, before sitting down with his newspaper, trying to calm down. Unwrapping the large Sunday newspaper, he stared at the front page.

"Is the Professor a Government Spy? Foul goings on at the Nuclear Processing Plant"

The article went on to suggest that the Professor could have been selling nuclear secrets to the Russians, as no ransom note had been found. Sources close to the Government had apparently hinted that that the reward of one million pounds had been officially sanctioned, and the newspaper concluded it was because he was wanted 'dead or alive' before he betrayed his country.

"Oh my god!" Len gasped. From reading this article it would seem that as soon as the Professor stepped foot outside his house he was likely to be shot on sight. What the hell were they going to do now?

He thought quickly. The gang would have to visit him tonight by railway, it would look too suspicious if they came in through his front door. Then another thought struck him. If he was being watched, maybe they were listening to his phone calls! There was only one thing for it, he would have to contact each man in person and warn them. Len glanced at the clock in the kitchen. The first train to New Romsey was not until 10.33 – another hour to wait. Len resisted the urge to go downstairs and check on the Professor. He was not in the mood to make chit chat and was too afraid of letting something slip.

The hour dragged by, but it gave Len time to make more plans. There was absolutely no point in the men coming round tonight if he could speak to them all personally and work out a way to get Mark to Downsend as soon as possible. He had already promised the man that he was going free on Monday, so something had to be sorted today.

He paced around his front room, thinking. The safest way would definitely be by train again, as early as possible. He checked his timetable. The timetable on Monday switched to purple, out of season. Which meant the trains no longer stopped at Romsey Sands! Added to which, the first train that left from New Romsey for Downsend was not until 10.30, and it was a 'request' only. That meant that unless somebody actually bought a ticket, the train did not run at all! There was nothing else for it, the only person who could help him now was George, the Station Master. He would have to go to New Romsey and throw himself on George's mercy.

At 10.30 Len boarded the *Southern Maiden*, which was being driven by Andy.

"Watcha," Andy called out as Len approached.

"Hello mate. I don't suppose you've seen Derek, Henry, Roy or Alan this morning?"

"Yeah, well I've seen Derek, anyway. He was off to the supermarket at Heath and he's back at one. Roy and Alan are only working this morning, I think, but I ain't seen them yet. Henry's at New Romsey all day."

"Oh right, cheers."

"Are you working later?"

"Me? Oh no, I'm off sick. Got a jiffy tummy. I just wanted to see what's going on and have a chat with the boys. I've been stuck inside for two days."

"I think there's a bug going round," replied Andy. "We're bound to catch something from all the people we meet."

"Yeah, probably right mate. Okay, I'd better get on board. We don't want to upset Henry." The men both laughed.

It was only a short ride to New Romsey but it seemed to take an eternity for Len. As soon as they arrived he planned to rush off in search of George. But by a stroke of luck, Henry was the Guard on the platform, and called out to him as he disembarked.

"Over here!" Henry shouted as Len climbed out of his carriage and stood up straight.

Len rushed over to speak to him. "Can I have a word in private," he hissed, aware that several people were hovering around within earshot.

"Right. Just a minute, I'll wave this train off."

Len waited for Henry to flag The Beetle away to Downsend, meanwhile looking around him in earnest. He felt very uncomfortable, as if all eyes were on him. Henry strolled back towards him as if he had not a care in the world, which was usually one of his good points but a bit irritating today, when Len was anxious to get back home as soon as possible.

"Is there somewhere private we can talk?"

"Okay, let's go in the café, but I can't be long, I'm on duty."

They moved through the throng of people all enjoying the sights and sounds of the Vintage weekend. Out of the corner of his eye, Len thought he saw somebody pointing in their direction.

"Come on, Henry, move a bit faster, I've got to get back!"

Henry finally caught Len's sense of urgency. The entered the café and immediately went into the private staff room, Len closing and bolting the door behind them.

"Is everything all right at home?"

"No it isn't, Henry. I'm being watched!"

"Are you sure you're not just being paranoid?"

"Positive! My newspaper boy saw two men questioning my home delivery driver, and then they took my receipts off him and started scrutinising them!"

"So how did you get here then, out the back way?"

"Sshh!" Len nodded, indicated they should lower their voices. "I've got to let him go."

"Already? What's the good of that?"

"Have you read the papers this morning?"

"No, why?"

"They're saying he's a traitor, wanted dead or alive."

"Oh, I see." Henry was silent for a moment. "This thing about being followed, I can't be sure but I think I was followed yesterday."

They both stared at each other in silence.

"They must be on to us!" Len whispered, louder than he meant to. "Look, whatever you do, don't come round to my place tonight."

"So what will you do? You can't let him go if they're going to shoot him."

"I don't know yet." Len looked miserable. "I'm going to ask George for his help."

"Oh no, you don't want to let George know about it."

"I've got no choice."

Henry shook his head and sighed. "It was never meant to come to this. Oh well, I suppose we can't keep hold of him for ever."

"You haven't seen him, he's losing his mind down in the Shed. He's like a caged animal."

"Right. Okay, you have to do what you have to do. If you need me to help, you'll have to get somebody to speak to me, then. We can't use the phones if they're monitoring us."

"No, that's what I thought. That's why I've come here. And if you see the others, can you tell them the same thing?"

"All right, will do. I'll keep my eyes open for them."

"Thanks, mate. Well, I'd better go and speak to George now."

"Good luck with that!"

"Okay. Next time I see you, hopefully it will all be over.

"Yes, fingers crossed. We'd better not leave this room together. I'll go out first, you wait a few minutes."

"No, I've got a better idea. Check that nobody's watching and then ask George to come in and see me."

"Right. Well, good luck again."

Len watched as Henry gave him a rueful smile before leaving and closing the door behind him. He waited anxiously as five minutes seemed to take an hour, before somebody tried to open the door, then knocked.

"Who is it?"

"It's George! Open up, you nitwit."

Len rushed to let him in, then bolted the door behind them.

"Tell me this isn't what I think it is," were George's first words.

"Oh. Well what do you think this is, then?"

"Tell me that it's got nothing to do with the Professor's disappearance. Tell me that I've got nothing to worry about with the Police asking for photographs of all my staff. Tell me, Len, because I really need to know."

Len looked embarrassed.

"Sounds like you've pretty much guessed."

"Oh no!" George spoke in hushed tones. "And is he where I think he is?"

Len nodded unhappily.

"What! He's all right, I take it?"

"Of course he is. We've got him chained up, though."

"Right. Sounds like I should be ringing the police right away, then."

"We only did it to save the railway." Len looked thoroughly miserable. "We never dreamt it would go this badly wrong. Please don't, George. We want to let him go; it's just a question of how to do it."

"So how on earth can I help with that?"

Len looked him squarely in the eyes.

"I need a train. Early tomorrow morning. It can stop outside my back yard and he can hide himself inside, then get out at Downsend."

"Well he might not agree to that. What's to stop him just walking outside and asking for help? I know the police are swarming all over the seafront."

"Soldiers, you mean. Armed with automatic rifles."

"So what's the difference with him getting out at Downsend?"

Len had already thought of this. "Somebody could pick him up and drive him to the power station. That way it would be safer for him. They wouldn't shoot him then, because he could tell them what's happened, and they would believe him."

"Why?"

Len shrugged his shoulders. "I dunno. I suppose they're his friends in there, the ones who turned up to meet him in the first place."

"I see." George sat down on one of the chairs and thought quietly for a moment. "I don't think you realise how many police – plain-clothed as well as in uniform – are swarming all over the place, Downsend included. And they're all looking out for your Professor."

"Oh." Len sounded disappointed, and they were both silent for a while.

"I've got an idea, Len, but I don't want to raise your hopes." He rubbed his chin thoughtfully. "I don't suppose he'd do it for me. He'd do it for a million pounds, though."

"Who's that?"

"I know somebody who works there. No, I'm not saying any more until I've spoken to him. He might be able to help, he might not. I'm thinking it would be better if you could get the Professor inside Downsend. Go back home and check that he's all right. You shouldn't have left him, really."

"I know, but ..."

"I'll get a message to you later on today about my plan, if this person agrees to do it. You'll get a note through the door. If you don't hear anything by 6 o'clock then you'll know it can't be done. Then you'll have to let the man go, in any case."

Len looked down. "I suppose so."

"I'm serious, Len. If you don't let him go, I'm going to have to tell the police myself."

"Okay. But how will you get the message to me?"

"I'll think of a way. You leave that to me. Now, you'd better catch the first train back."

"Thank you, George. Thanks very much!" Len unlocked the staffroom door and they both headed back to the station, Len boarding the first train going home.

CHAPTER NINETEEN
Alan's Tale

ALAN had been busy shunting *Captain Jack* back into the sheds on Sunday morning when he had noticed a small group of people watching him. It looked like a family group of an older man, two old women, and a family with young sons. He smiled and waved at them but none of them waved back, not even the boys. When he had finished reversing he jumped off the locomotive and walked back down the platform, expecting to see them still there, but they had vanished. This was a bit strange but it did not worry him unduly. There were hundreds of other families only too happy to smile and wave at him today.

Shortly after, a red-faced George came over to him just as he was about to climb another engine. He looked around before saying in a low voice,

"Don't go round Len's tonight."

Alan was speechless for a few seconds as a feeling of panic gripped him. "Oh right, any reason?"

George gave him a knowing look. "That's the message. In fact, you can go home now, if you like."

Alan had the feeling that he was being told off like a naughty schoolboy. He didn't know that George was red-faced because he had just directed the group of witnesses over in Alan's direction, and from the look on their faces when they came back it seemed as if at least one of them had recognised him. He didn't know that George had the horrible feeling that Alan's days of freedom were numbered, which is why he wanted to send him home to be with his family for as long as possible.

Too frightened to ask any more questions, Alan replied, "Okay," before walking out of the main entrance and getting into his car. It was another five minutes before he managed to drive out of the car park and back down Smallstone Road to his house.

"Hello, Alan!" Linda, his wife, remarked when he walked in. "I wasn't expecting you for another couple of hours. Is everything all right?"

"I'm not sure. George just sent me home."

"Really? That's very odd." Linda looked perplexed, then said, "What have you been up to?"

Alan laughed. His wife always knew instinctively when something was up.

"Nothing," he answered casually. "I don't suppose you've heard from Len?"

"No, nobody's rung."

Alan tried Len's phone, but there was no answer.

"I'm glad you're home early, we can go shopping before it gets too manic."

He gave a mock sigh. "I knew you'd say that. Come on then, we might as well go now."

Linda rushed to get ready before Alan changed his mind. This was too good an opportunity to miss. The Saints supermarket was always jam-packed on a Sunday afternoon so the earlier they could get there, the better.

It was a struggle to drive even the short distance up Smallstone Road to the roundabout and the supermarket turnoff, what with vintage buses and cars chugging up and down, but it was a pretty sight to see. Luckily, most of the day-trippers had come armed with their own supplies or else they hadn't discovered the local supermarket yet. Alan noted that the aisles were busy but not packed. Why his wife had to do the shopping on a Sunday when they had all week to do it he never knew, and it caused countless arguments. It was one of those routines that she had got into. Sometimes they would go for a carvery in the high street first if the store looked too busy, so it was not always a chore. Alan secretly thought it was just a ruse to get him away from the railway

112

and have some of his attention at the weekends, so he went along with it.

They had been in the store for about twenty minutes when Alan first suspected that something was wrong. A couple of men with a large trolley seemed to be following them around the aisle and not doing any shopping, apart from a token pre-packed sandwich in their cart.

"You don't know those two, do you?" he whispered to his wife.

Never one to be discreet, she turned round and stared at them both. "No, I don't think so."

"Stand here a minute and let them go past."

They waited for the two men to finally go past, still with nothing added to the trolley.

"They don't look gay," he hissed, after they had wheeled past them.

"Shush, Alan!

He watched as they reached the top of the aisle, waiting to see where they went next. The men hesitated as if they were unsure where to go next, before turning left. Alan quickly reversed his trolley and wheeled it back in the opposite direction, before turning to his left. Sure enough, after a few minutes the two men were back in the same aisle as they were.

"See what I mean, they're following us!"

"Well I don't see why they would do that. I'm going to ask them."

"No you don't, get back here!"

It was too late, Linda was already upon them.

"You're not following us, are you?" she asked in a slightly jokey tone.

"Er no, of course not," one of the men replied, sounding like he'd been caught out.

"No, I didn't think you would be. Well, that's a relief. Alan, it's all right, they're not following us." With that she walked back to him.

Alan was as red as a beetroot and laughed nervously as he looked around. No one else seemed to be taking much notice, thankfully.

"Come on, Linda, let's get out of here," he said to her, steering her towards the tills.

"I've only got half the shopping!" she protested, as he continued to push the trolley towards the exits.

As they waited in the queue, Alan noted that the two men had joined an adjacent line even though all they had was a pre-packed sandwich and two cans of coke, and they could have joined the "five items or less" queue several aisles down.

"They're still following us," he hissed to her. "Come on, let's go home."

"What?"

"No, don't say anything, pretend you haven't noticed. Let them leave first."

Alan allowed the person behind to go in front of them, even though they had nearly as many items in their trolley. Linda started to look a bit worried as the two men, who had gone through the checkout, seemed to be hanging around at the exit.

"I think you're right," she hissed. "Shall we call Security?"

"No, no, don't do that! Look, I've got a plan. We'll head towards the exit and then we'll dive into the toilets."

"What, with all our shopping?" Linda turned her nose up.

"Just listen a minute! You know by the toilets they've got a goods lift? Well, I'm going to disappear in there and go up to the top floor and get out that way. Meanwhile, you hang around in the Ladies until you've heard the lift reach the top and the doors open, then you come back outside again and wait for around five minutes. Meanwhile I'll be making my way out of the store by the loading bay round the back and I'll cross over the road and wait for you by the bus stop."

"So what do I do then?"

"After about 5-10 minutes, leave the store and drive to the bus stop. Don't look round at the men; just drive straight to the bus stop and pick me up. Give me enough time to get there, though."

"But why should they be following us, Alan? Can't we call the Police?"

"Linda, I think they are the Police."

"Oh no! Why, what have you done?" She was, by now, quite distraught.

"Don't worry about that for now, I'll explain later. Just do what I say!"

"Okay," she replied reluctantly, as they approached the toilets.

"Ready? Right, now!"

The plan worked like clockwork. Alan ran inside the goods lift and drew the door shut before pressing the up arrow. Linda waited until the lift started moving before she rushed inside the Ladies with four bags of shopping, and waited. A few minutes later she heard voices, and was sure that the two men had gone into the Gents to look for Alan. She waited a good while before peering cautiously outside, and seeing no-one there went back outside. She caught sight of the men standing at the cigarette kiosk, watching her.

Linda stuck to the plan. For all the men knew, Alan could be inside the disabled toilet. After a few more minutes she picked up her bags of shopping and walked hurriedly to their car. She felt the men behind her but she didn't look back, throwing the bags onto the rear seat and quickly starting up the car. She then drove over a stretch of grass which was a short cut to the road, before pulling out in front of the traffic lights and zooming round the roundabout, heading for the bus stop. Looking back in her wing mirror she could see that there was a red car stuck behind a Saints delivery lorry waiting at the traffic lights. Result! She hurriedly pulled up and barely waited as Alan jumped inside the car and slammed the door shut.

"Well done!" said Alan breathlessly as he pulled on his seat belt.

"I'm not leading them back to our house," Linda told him. "I'm going to the pub, and you can jolly well tell me what this is all about!"

Alan knew then that game was up, and he would have to tell her everything. He also realised that something had gone horribly wrong with their master plan.

CHAPTER TWENTY
Roy's Story

Roy had been busy enjoying himself in the machine room on Sunday morning when George telephoned and asked him to come into the shop. When he had arrived there was a group of people standing by the desk.

"Don't let me interrupt," he said, panting a little.

"No, that's okay." George looked a little embarrassed. "I just wanted to ask you to take this package back to the machine room; it's a part that we've been waiting for."

"For *Dark Prince*? Blimey, that was quick."

"Yes, good service, isn't it? You can use it straight away and get the train moving again; it's blocking one of the points."

"Right then, I'll do that now."

"Thanks a lot."

"Okay, see you later, George." Roy rushed back to the machine room to open his parcel.

After he left a policewoman, who had been hiding out of view, came over and spoke to the group. "Don't say anything yet, we'll talk outside."

One of the older women nodded.

"Thanks very much for your help, Mr Cuthbert. We'll be back this afternoon."

George nodded and gave a rueful smile. He was starting to feel like Judas Iscariot. His only consolation was that Roy would open the parcel and read the message he had hastily hidden inside.

This afternoon he very much suspected he would have to the same charade with Derek. George sighed heavily. Derek was his favourite member of staff.

When Roy opened his parcel he found an old spanner with a note sellotaped round it. It read, "DO NOT GO TO

LEN'S TONIGHT UNDER ANY CIRCUMSTANCES. Wait 10 minutes then meet me in the Café staff room".

"Oh heck!" Roy hastily got his things together, then paced the engine room for ten minutes before making for the Café.

"All I can tell you is that Len came to see me this morning to ask for my help," George said, in response to his earnest questioning.

Roy looked down at the floor. "So you know about it, then?"

"Not exactly, but I know that you are involved as well."

"Did Len tell you that?"

"No, it's nothing to do with Len. I can't tell you how I know, but I do."

"I see."

"I want you to go home and ask your wife to call round here at five o'clock."

"Why's that? I don't want Carol involved."

George beckoned him closer. "I've got to get an urgent message to Len before six tonight, and she's the only person I can think of to deliver it."

"Can't you ring him?"

"No, I can't. And I'd advise you not to, either."

"Right." Roy paused, then lowered his voice. "So why can't I go round there?"

"Len's being watched," George replied quietly.

He handed Roy a pile of RHLR leaflets. "What I thought was, Carol could pretend to be delivering leaflets. You live just around the corner from Len. When she gets to his house she can post my message through his letterbox, as well."

Roy considered this. "I see. So what's this message?"

"I don't know yet. I've got to ask somebody a favour. I'll know by five o'clock, and I'll write Len a message. Like I said, we can't ring him; but he still needs to know whether I can help him or not."

Roy paused and considered the options. "And there's nobody else you can ask?"

"Well can you think of somebody? I can't. What if they decided to open the letter up and hand it to the Police? Don't forget, there's a lot of money being offered for information."

"What if I'm being followed as well?"

"You probably are, but I doubt they're watching Carol. Where is she now?"

"She was supposed to be going to Linda's, I think."

"What's her number? I'll give her a call."

"07705-379826, if she's got it switched on."

"Okay, I'll call and you can speak to her."

When her phone rang Carol answered it immediately. George passed it over to Roy.

"Oh hello love, it's me. Are you at Linda's?"

"Hello, Roy, no – I was just about to leave when she rang and said that Alan had been sent home early and they were going shopping."

"Okay. Carol, I'm going to ask you to do me a favour, love. You don't have to if you don't want to."

"Of course, what is it? Is everything all right?"

"Don't say anything over the phone," George hissed.

"Do you think you could come in to the station and speak to George?"

"Your boss George?"

"Yes, that's right."

"Are you all right?" she asked again.

"Yes, I'm fine." Roy started to get choked up. "Look, I can't tell you over the phone, love, if you could just come in, George can explain."

"Are you sure you're all right?" There was the sound of panic in her voice.

"Yes, I'm fine. It's just that we need your help with something, that's all."

"Oh, okay. I'll come right away."

"Don't rush, love. It's not that important."

"Okay, see you in five minutes, 'bye." She hung up.

Roy started getting red in the face as he paced the floor. "B***s, I wish we'd never started this now. The last thing I want is for Carol to get arrested!"

George sat down in one of the chairs and indicated that he should sit down, too.

"Look, Roy, I'm trying my hardest to get that man out of Len's house without anybody seeing him go. And with any luck I can get him actually inside the power station. That's the best I can do, I'm afraid. Whether he then decides to tell the police what happened, that's up to him."

"That would be brilliant …"

They stopped suddenly. Outside could be heard the sounds of raucous shouting and cheering. They both looked outside cautiously.

"Go on, my son!" shouted one of the drivers.

They saw that a small crowd had gathered around a television screen mounted on the wall in the corner. In full view was an official-looking photograph of Derek.

"Police have warned that he is very dangerous and not to be approached. If anyone sees him they should call 999 immediately…"

"Hooray!" followed by another round of cheers.

"What on earth's happened?" George asked, dreading the answer.

"It's Derek! He's decked two policemen and he's gone on the run!" replied Andy, who was on his lunch break. "I only saw him a few hours ago; must have happened soon after that."

"Did he say where he was going?" asked Roy.

"To Dial's, as far as I know. Maybe he was caught shoplifting?"

There was a bout of laughter.

"All right, everyone, let's not blacken Derek's name without knowing what's happened," said George. "And as it seems we're going to be short of staff this afternoon, if anyone can work a few extra hours, I'd be grateful."

"I'll do Derek's shift," said Andy.

"Thanks, Andy. I still need another person, though."

"Okay, I'll stay as well."

"Cheers, Brian. I'd appreciate that. And if there's any more updates on Derek, can you let me know?"

In answer to this question there were more cheers and laughter from the small crowd. Roy, however, did not look happy.

"One down, four to go," he mumbled with a resigned shrug. "Let's just hope we don't get our wives arrested, too.

Ten minutes later Carol showed up at the front desk, where Roy and George were waiting. She looked relieved to see her husband in one piece.

"Right, keep her here until I get back," George ordered. "If anyone asks, I've gone to lunch."

He headed straight to his daughter's house in Smallstone, where, if luck was in, her husband, Gary, would be home for lunch. As he pulled up outside he noticed his son-in-law's work's van parked in the drive. Gary had a nice little business looking after vending machines in the area, working mainly at Downsend. He would refill the coffee machines with plastic cups and sort out any problems with the machines, as well as putting sandwiches and chocolate bars into the revolving vending machines for staff working out of hours.

George was not overly keen on Gary, feeling he wasn't good enough for Julie, his only daughter, but they'd been together for years and married for three, although no children as yet.

"Hello Dad," said Julie, the surprise in her voice. "Didn't expect to see you today?"

"Hello daught," he replied with her pet name. "I've just popped in to see Gary, if he's here."

Julie looked even more surprised. "Yes, he's having a bite for lunch. Well come in, then."

Gary looked up from the front room as they walked in. "Hello Dad, is everything all right?"

"Yes, everything's fine, carry on eating. I'd just like to put something to you when you've finished."

"Car broken down again?"

"No, nothing like that. I'll go in the other room while you eat your lunch."

Julie made them all a cup of tea and fussed around, insisting on making her father a sandwich. "What's it all about?" she asked. "Come on, something's up."

"Well if you must know, I'm going to ask Gary to give a lift to somebody into work tomorrow."

"Oh, that's all right then. I'm sure Gary won't mind."

George didn't answer, concentrating on his sandwich.

After a few minutes Gary came into the kitchen with his empty plate. "What was that about a lift?"

"Yes, a friend of mine wants to get to Downsend tomorrow and I wondered if you could give them a lift. Only it'll be early in the morning."

"How early? I start work at eight."

"That should be fine. You don't have to do it if you don't want to. Are you going back to work now?"

"Just about to, yes."

"I'll explain more outside."

"All right, then." He raised puzzled eyebrows to his wife, who shrugged back.

George said goodbye to his daughter and waited until they were out of earshot. "How do you fancy a million pounds?"

"Do what?" he laughed incredulously.

"I'm trying to get the missing professor back inside Downsend."

"Are you serious? What, that one they keep going on about on the telly?"

"That's right. We can take him on the train as far as Downsend but we don't want the police to get hold of him. So I was hoping you could take him inside in your van. You must have a pass to get in there."

"Oh no, don't get me involved in that. The whole place is swarming with armed soldiers and god knows what else."

"All you have to say is that you saw him wandering up the road and he flagged you down for a lift. He can get into the back of your van."

"Well, can't he walk from Downsend Station?"

"No, not if he doesn't want the police to get to him. They've been told he's a traitor. He's not. He was kidnapped by – somebody ..."

"You kidnapped him?"

"Not me, no, I knew nothing about it until yesterday. So now they want to let him go, but they're scared that they're going to shoot the poor man first and ask questions later. I thought you might be able to help. There's the reward, at the end of the day."

Gary rubbed his chin.

"I wouldn't be able to drive up by the seafront because they've got roadblocks top and bottom. And there's plenty of policemen by the railway station, 'cos I've seen them there today."

"What about the rail crossing before you get to Downsend, on Downsend Road? We could stop the train there instead?"

"Hmm, well I haven't seen any roadblocks there. I suppose it's possible."

"We could get him there for half seven." George could tell that Gary was getting more interested.

"I know exactly where to take him when we get inside. I have to walk right past the investigation room to get to the canteen." He laughed. "I'll take him straight in and claim my million pounds!"

"Yes, that's it. You found him wandering around the marsh totally lost, no idea where he is, and he asks you to take him to Downsend, and Bob's your uncle!"

"Okay, I'll be there. Better not say anything to Julie, though."

"No, I wouldn't if I were you. Still, if you do change your mind before tomorrow, just let me know. Okay, son?"

"All right, Dad, see you at 7.30 tomorrow."

"I'd better be getting back to the station now," George smiled, giving his daughter a wave before getting back into his car.

Don't be late!" Gary laughed.

They both knew this was a joke. George was a stickler for timekeeping.

CHAPTER TWENTY-ONE
The Professor Escapes

WHEN the Professor woke on Sunday morning he knew one thing for sure, he had to get out of this dungeon before he lost his mind completely. He had been working hard for hours on end during the night, using the bicycle chain to pull and grind away on the pipe that was keeping him down in this hell-hole. This morning he started again and it finally seemed to be working. He had found a joint which looked particularly rusty and had been focusing his efforts on that, and it was started to loosen up. Another night's work and he was sure he could break free. But then he would still have to get past Len.

Much as Mark had tried to avoid forming a bond with his kidnapper, it had started to happen. He now cared about Len and his unhappy love life. He even cared about the railway. And if he was honest, he didn't want Len to spend the rest of his dotage in prison. He even felt some sympathy for Derek, the thug who had attacked him; he had seen for himself how easy it was to descend into animal behaviour and act instinctively.

"I'm sure I have also been damaged by this experience," he thought, considering his options for the hundredth time. "The best thing I can do is to get Len drunk again – really drunk. I'll make sure the chain is loose first, get Len drunk and then escape. If they ask me where I've been, I'm sure I can pretend to have had a nervous breakdown. I think I'm on the edge of one, anyway."

Mark gave the chain another yank, and a horrible creaking sound ensued. The pipe was moving! Just at that moment he heard the sound of Len opening up the hatch, and he threw himself back down on the couch and pretended to be asleep. He listened carefully as Len clambered down the rungs and tiptoed down the steps, placing a flask and plate of food on the table next to him, before climbing back upstairs. To his disappointment, he heard him pull the bolt across the entrance.

He waited another five minutes before starting to pull on his ankle chain again. It took a further ten minutes to wear away the joint. With a final jerk, the pipe swung out from the wall and faced towards him. Mark quietly slipped the chain off the end of the pipe and untangled it from his foot. He was free! The first thing he did was to creep quietly up the stairs and test the door, but it was securely locked. He started to feel a sense of panic, and a wheeze rose in his chest. Oh no, not now. It had been strange how his asthma had not troubled him since he was kidnapped, almost as if his body had gone into survival mode. But the thought of being trapped was making his chest burn, and the familiar hyperventilating returned.

Mark went back to the couch and took several puffs from his inhaler, trying to breathe normally. He took a few sips of water and then breathed into his cupped hands to try to calm down. Thankfully, it seemed to be working. A few minutes later he heard a door slam and the faint sound of crunching gravel. Great! Len had finally left the house. His asthma seemed to stop as suddenly as it had started.

Five minutes later a train roared overhead, the noise emanating from left to right. Mark thought carefully back to the day before. According to Len, left was towards Downsend, right was for New Romsey, which is where he must be heading. Now it was time to make plans. At first, it was good enough just to walk around his prison cell, stretching his legs and easing the stiffness in his back. Then Mark went to the bar area and helped himself to a double brandy and coke, hiding the glass afterwards. He started to relax, and immediately felt more optimistic and in control. He tried pushing the hatch with all his strength, but nothing

126

budged. Holding both hands onto the rungs, he tried to kick it, to no effect. The trouble was there was only a small landing at the top of the stairs and the hatch was too high above it, so you couldn't get a good push at it.

Mark paced around searching for something to use as a tool. A bar stool seemed a good bet. He climbed a couple of rungs on the ladder and rammed it again and again against the hatch. It made a great noise but did not appear to be doing anything. He searched behind the bar and found a cigarette lighter. He could take a chance and set the door alight, but most likely his asthma would finish him off before the door burnt down. Mark looked around and considered carefully. Maybe the metal pipe would be suitable, if he could break it free. Eventually he managed to pull the broken section off the wall, and tried to use it as a battering ram. It was making a good mess of the inside of the hatch but it was sharp, cutting his hands. Defeated, he had to pause and recover his breath.

Mark sat back on the sofa and switched on the remote. They were reviewing the Sunday papers on the morning chat show, and it seemed like he was still headline news. But the headlines were not very reassuring.

"*Was the Professor a Government Spy?*" screamed the Herald.

"*Wanted Dead or Alive!*" declared the Sunday Lighthouse.

He put his head in his hands. From the sounds of the commentators, they were very much of the opinion that Mark had gone into hiding, possibly carrying some top-secret documents. It was not looking good. He picked up his briefcase and looked at the diagrams inside their plastic wallets. No doubt they were covered in the fingerprints of his kidnappers. And it was obvious that this briefcase was no longer secure. At 11 o'clock one of the presenters said that an update had been received on the missing professor, and they were heading over to the newsdesk for a newsflash. Mark gasped. A photo of his attacker, Derek, appeared full screen. The newscaster said that Derek Barton should not be approached under any circumstances but that anybody seeing him should dial 999. Mark was suddenly elated.

"Yes!"

Then he realised that this did not necessarily put him in the clear. Derek's fingerprints may well be on his plastic wallets or his briefcase. They might think that Derek had made off with one of his diagrams, with his consent. He checked through his briefcase. The diagrams were all there. He knew that. But would they believe him? Could they have been copied? He certainly didn't like the look of images of the helicopters and police dogs that seemed to be scouring the area nearby, not to mention armed soldiers. Mark was suddenly unsure what to do next.

An ominous rumbling sound overhead from right to left announced a train heading back from New Romsey to Downsend. The only thing Mark could think of doing was to place the pipe back into position and pretend that he was still chained up. Then next time Len came down the steps he could push him out of the way and make a dash for freedom. The urge to escape was so tempting that he didn't feel able to resist, whatever the outcome. If he had to leave the plans in the dungeon, so be it!

Listening carefully, he heard the back door open and then slam shut. Footsteps overhead. After a few minutes, he heard the bolt draw back and saw Len emerging through the hatch at the top of the stairs.

"Good news, Mark!" he called out. "We're going to get you out of here. We might even be able to get you inside Downsend, how about that?"

Mark watched as Len came down the stairs. He waited for Len to head towards the bar area and then suddenly bolted towards the exit.

"Bloody hell! Mark! Don't go out there, they'll shoot you!"

Len came running up the stairs after him, but Mark was too quick. He virtually flew up the metal ladder and climbed through the entrance. Len was at the bottom of the ladder, trying to grab his feet. He quickly pulled himself up and through before pushing the wooden hatch back to the floor and securing the bolt, laughing deliriously. He was free!

"They're watching the house, Mark. They've got guns! Read the newspaper, if you don't believe me!"

He ran towards the windows while Len continued to shout through the door. He stared through the net curtains and made out a red car sitting opposite with two men inside. Just at that moment he realised that a helicopter was very close by. It sounded as if it was circling overhead, making quite a racket. He felt his chest tightening up again.

"Mark! You've got to take your plans with you. I was going to give you my suitcase. Mark! You can't leave me here!"

He heard the fear in Len's voice. Ha! He was giving him a taste of his own medicine; revenge was sweet. Heading towards the back door, his eyes caught the newspaper headlines.

"I suppose I'd better read this," he thought grimly, as Len continued to shout through the door. The article was not very reassuring. He felt a growing sense of anger as he read through the article.

"Soviet spy? I've given the best part of my life to them and the first conclusion they jump to is I'm a traitor!"

When he couldn't bear to read any more he threw the newspaper on the floor then paced up and down, trying to clear his head. It was hard to think properly with the sound of the helicopter whirring overhead. He spotted an old briefcase on the floor. Maybe Len really was trying to help him? Maybe it would be better if he were smuggled inside the compound. And he could take all the plans out of their wallets and put them in Len's briefcase, as if nothing had ever happened to them. Just at that point the droning noise of the helicopter seemed to fade away.

"All right, Len," he called out by the hatch, "Tell me how you were going to get me inside?"

"My friend knows someone who works there. Probably in his van, I'm not too sure. They're letting me know tonight. Honestly!"

"What time tonight?"

"By six o'clock, he said." Len paused. "And he said that if he couldn't help, I've got to set you free anyway."

"Right. I'll have to think about it." Mark paced the kitchen floor some more, considering his options. "How are they going to let you know?"

"They're putting a note through the door. If there's no note, they can't help."

"I see. Well, here's what I'll do. I'm going to keep you down there until six o'clock, and then I'm going to read the note, if there is one. If I like what it says, I might agree to it. If I don't like it, then I'm out of here. Do you understand?"

"What, you're keeping me locked down here till six o'clock?"

"Yes!"

"You can't do that! What about food?"

"Well, there's packets of crisps and peanuts down there, that should do. And a bucket!"

"What about your diagrams?"

"I'll worry about that after I've read the note."

There was some mumbling from Len and he heard him going back downstairs. After a short time he came back up.

"I'll set fire to them! If you don't let me out I'm going to destroy your diagrams."

"No, don't do that!" The words came out automatically.

"I'm going to. I'm going to do it right now." His voice tailed off as he opened the Professor's battered briefcase. "Oh yes, let me see. 'Phase I – Commissioning'. That's a pretty diagram, did you do it yourself?"

Mark was silent.

"I'm just setting it alight now. Can you see the smoke?"

There came the sound of the cigarette lighter clicking, something burning and the smell of smoke, which wafted up through the hatch.

"Stop it! You've no idea what you're doing!"

"Nearly gone now, I'm afraid. Onto number two."

"All right! I'll let you out, if you bring my suitcase with you! But I'm not going back down there, and if you try anything I'm walking right out of here and you'll be in prison before you know it." Mark drew back the bolt and lifted the hatch.

Len felt a surge of relief, and made sure he climbed through tactically so as Mark couldn't grab hold of his case. The Professor was also relieved when he realised Len had only set light to some packaging, and his diagrams were still in one piece.

"Why you...!" Mark left the words unsaid, as he checked his lifetime's work.

They both stood and looked at each other, on equal footing for the first time, then they both started laughing.

"You had me going there," laughed the Professor. "You shouldn't have done that, I might have had a seizure!"

"So might I, at the thought of being stuck down there! Nobody would have found me, I told them not to come round because I'm being watched. In fact, you should stay clear of the windows if you don't want to be seen. Who knows what sort of lens they could peer in with."

Len handed Mark his old briefcase. "I know it's not leather, but it's all I've got."

The professor sat down at the table in the kitchen and transferred his diagrams one by one into the new case, carefully removing each one from its plastic pocket.

"You should destroy my old case and all these wallets after I'm gone."

"Right. Yes, I never thought of that."

The professor sighed, but continued putting them in his new case.

"Do you want a cup of tea while you're doing that?"

"Oh yes please, Len."

"I don't suppose you're going to tell me what it's all about – this million pound reward and all these helicopters and stuff?"

"This," the professor said solemnly, "is my life's work. And believe it or not, this is the only copy of my new invention. The only other place it remains is in my head. And that's debatable, after receiving your friend's fists to it."

Len looked sheepish. "Well, sorry about that, Mark. You know we didn't really understand the implications of what we were doing."

"Quite." He continued to rearrange his diagrams in order. "That should be it. Now, do you have a key for this?"

"Did have, but that's long gone, I'm afraid." Len placed a mug of tea on the table next to Mark, along with a bag of sugar and a spoon. He glanced at the kitchen clock. "Only one o'clock. What on earth are we going to do until six?"

"Well, I suggest you put the television on. Do you know your friend Derek's gone on the run?"

"No! Oh my god. Was it on the news?"

"It certainly was. It said he'd attacked two policemen and gone on the run. 'Not to be approached under any circumstances'."

"More like he sussed out he was being followed, and decked them both." Len shook his head. "You've got to admit, that's something of an achievement, fighting off two SAS men probably half his age."

"Yes, I stood no chance, did I?" Mark gave an ironic laugh. "I suppose that makes me feel a little better. Now," he said, closing the case and wiping it with a tea towel, "do not touch this briefcase again!"

The men both sat in the kitchen and chatted while they waited. Something was posted through the letterbox at three o'clock, which Len rushed to pick up and take through to the kitchen.

"I want to read it first!" Mark demanded.

"Oh, okay." Len handed it over reluctantly.

He examined it carefully. It appeared to be two railway leaflets stuck together, which he managed to pull apart carefully. Inside was a note which he read out:

"Tomorrow, be ready for the train at 7 o'clock."

"Game on!" exclaimed Len. "Well, Mark, what do you say? Are you up for it?"

"Yes!" he replied. "I will finally complete my journey to Downsend. Justice is served."

"You might have to get in someone's van as well."

"That's okay. It can't be any worse than being in your hole."

"*The Shed*, Mark! I suggest we face our fears and go back down there to celebrate."

"Deal!" he replied.

CHAPTER TWENTY-TWO
Mason Returns

PETER MASON was not a happy man. From the telephone conversation he'd just had with his deputy, Craig, all hell had broken loose this Sunday morning, and it looked like Craig was to blame. By all accounts he had taken it upon himself to order a dawn raid on Dr Wells' farmhouse without asking his permission, and had managed to upset Dr Wells, his wife, three children and his elderly mother, who had been staying in the annex. Then Dr Wells had been arrested and taken to HQ for questioning. However, he was refusing to speak to anyone except for Mason, which is why he was now being driven post-haste from London to Downsend.

Added to which, Mason had had words with the Sussex Police and Crime Commissioner, including an official complaint about the number of front doors which had been broken down in the search for the Professor in the Romsey area, resulting in numerous upset little old ladies and a possible heart-attack for one elderly gentleman. The holiday park were also unhappy with the harassment of their visitors. The whole thing had been too heavy-handed and was now a complete shambles. Mason had been forced to apologise for Craig's actions and had already resolved to remove him from the case.

To add to Mason's disappointment, he had just spent a pleasant evening with his daughter Becky, and she had even agreed to stay the night at his apartment in London. It was extremely annoying to think that he'd had to leave at the crack of dawn without getting the chance to explain to her what was wrong; just a scribbled apology under her bedroom door. On a Sunday, as well. Bad timing all round! He arrived back at Downsend just after 9am.

"I just don't know what you were thinking of!" Mason exploded, as soon as he saw Craig. "Dr Wells let's us have the run of his offices and facilities, and this is how we treat him. Now he's refusing to come back to work until he's been assured you've left the premises! I appreciate we had some concerns and we wanted some questions answered, but as for raiding his house – I'm speechless!"

"Well the evidence all pointed to a conspiracy, with him as the ringleader."

"So he's got the Professor all tied up in his outhouse, with his wife and children next door? You can't seriously have believed that?"

"Not by itself, sir, but …"

"And now, if he has got the Professor tied up elsewhere, we're never going to find him, are we?"

"Aerial support flew over his property and identified that there was somebody in the annex and they weren't moving, and when taken with the other evidence…"

"Being what, exactly?"

"The telephone calls to the railway two weeks before the Professor's visit."

"He's already told us that he arranged for the Professor to travel by railway." Mason was trying to stop himself from shouting, but was not succeeding.

"And his mobile phone – he sent a text from his phone while actually at New Romsey Station, on the Sunday before Professor Hills disappeared."

"Really? Saying what?"

"*I've got the present, where are you?*"

"Right." Mason paused for a moment. "Well, I admit that is interesting. Have you asked him about this?"

"Yes, sir. That's when he went very quiet and said that he would speak to no-one else except you."

"I see. Well, I'd better go and see what he's got to say about it all. Meanwhile, Craig, I'm afraid I'm going to have to release you from the case."

"But Sir!"

"No, I'm sorry, Craig, this has gone too far. I've had complaints about you from the Sussex Police Commissioner this morning, so I've got no choice. Report to HR on Monday morning."

Craig looked crestfallen, but collected his things from the office and left without another word. He realised that his career with MI8 was over.

After waiting a decent while for Craig to leave the building, Mason headed for Dr Wells' office, which is where he had been detained. Two police officers were guarding the door, which they unlocked after Mason showed his ID. Dr Wells looked up dejectedly as he walked in, then stood up and started shouting.

"Mr Mason, I can't believe you would suspect me of being involved in Mark's disappearance! And as for that deputy of yours organising a dawn raid, he nearly finished us all off, let alone my mother. She's 85, for God's sake! If she suffers any ill health because of this, I'll be suing you to Kingdom come!"

"No, I'm very sorry and I must apologise for my Deputy's actions, they were extremely misguided. If it's any consolation, he has been removed from the case."

"I should think so, too!" replied Dr Wells indignantly.

Mason paused. "He did tell me, however, that you wanted to speak to me about the telephone call that you made at the train station."

"Ah yes, the one about the 'present'." He sat back down again. "You see, Mr Mason, I've remembered something. I'm sorry that I didn't think of it sooner, as it may be relevant to Mark's disappearance."

"Please, go on."

Dr Wells took a sip of water.

"As I've already told you, on the day that Mark went missing I was at Downsend Station with two of my colleagues waiting for him to arrive. When he wasn't on the train I spoke to the driver and asked if anything untoward had happened on the journey, and I said 'hello' to him because I recognised him from the week before."

"Really? From a trip to New Romsey Station?"

"Yes, that's right. I'd been given some vouchers to have a go at driving one of the steam trains as a present for Father's Day but I hadn't got round to using them until last week. And it was the same driver and the same train that I'd been on, that Mark went missing from."

"Are you sure about that?"

"Positive! The driver's name was Len, and it was the *Green Dawn*."

"I see. I'll just write that down so that I can have it checked out. That really was a coincidence." Mason pulled out a notepad and jotted something down. "So who were you sending the message to?"

"My mother. My wife dropped me off at the station and I was supposed to be meeting her and my sons there, but I couldn't find them. I exchanged my voucher at the shop and then gave mother a call. They were sitting in the café, waiting for me."

"Right. And her number is?"

"07763 181273."

Mason wrote it down.

"Thanks very much, Dr Wells." He was about to leave but there was something about his demeanour which had changed. "Is that everything you wanted to tell me?"

There was a pregnant pause. "I've remembered something else."

"I see." Mason waited.

"I was a little drunk that day, I'm ashamed to admit."

137

Mason remained silent.

"I may have said something to the driver."

"Something about the Professor?"

"Yes."

Another pause. Mason waited patiently.

"I may have said something along the lines of, 'you'll be having an important visitor on Friday', something like that."

"Right. It's a pity you didn't remember this before, Dr Wells."

"Yes, I realise that now, but honestly, until he asked me about that text it had gone completely from my mind."

"So what did this driver – Len –say? Please try to remember exactly, if you would."

"I can't remember word for word, but it was something like, 'Is it something to do with what's in the papers', or words to that effect."

"And what did he mean by that?"

"Well, they had been discussing about the nuclear processing plant and storing the country's nuclear waste under Romsey Marsh."

"Oh yes, I see. And that may have possibly affected the railway – digging up the tracks, that kind of thing?"

"It definitely would have, yes."

"Right." Mason stood up immediately. "Thank you very much for this information, Dr Wells, I'll get onto it right away." He turned to leave. "Oh, and if the telephone message checks out, I don't see any reason to keep you here. If you wouldn't mind waiting while I get onto it."

"Of course, fair enough. I repeat, I'm sorry I didn't remember it sooner."

"Okay, we won't worry about that now. I'm going to check the driver's statement and take it from there. I'll be back as soon as I can."

"Yes, let's hope it helps you to find Mark. I'll never forgive myself if they've done anything to him."

Mason did not respond but left the room, closing the door behind him. He went to his office and was surprised to see DCI Willis sitting at his desk. He saw the man's confusion, who stood up.

"Sorry sir, you must be Mr Mason. I'm DCI Willis.

"Hello, yes, I'm Peter Mason." They shook hands. "They've put you here as well, have they?"

"Yes. Craig, said I could use it as there was nowhere else available."

"I see; no problem." He paused. "Actually, Craig's desk in HQ is available if you'd like it, as he's no longer working on the project."

"Oh, right."

Mason knew that Willis was waiting for him to elaborate, but he was not forthcoming.

"Well in that case, I'll get my things together and move there."

"No, sit down, don't worry about that right now. You may actually be able to help me out. I'm looking for a copy of one of the witness statements – the train driver, somebody called Len?"

"Ah yes, a Mr Len Sutton, I remember that name." Willis rifled through the paperwork on his desk. "Here it is."

Mason scanned the brief statement rapidly. "Aha! This is very interesting. Sutton said that he was driving the *Southern Maiden*. I've just been told that it was the *Green Dawn*."

"Really? Kind of ironic, don't you think? Saving the area from becoming a nuclear dumping ground, possibly?"

"Yes, that's it! He was trying to deflect the connection. And Mr Sutton knew about the Professor being on the train, according to Dr Wells, who has just admitting telling him."

"So he must be the ringleader," mused Willis. "Presuming Dr Wells didn't tell anyone else."

"That's right," Mason agreed. "Sutton must have told the others and set the whole thing in motion. What do we know about this Mr Sutton? Has his house been searched?"

"Yes, I believe it was one of the first properties searched, if I remember correctly." Willis looked at his notebook. "That's right. Craig told me that all the properties along the Parade had been searched because they backed onto the railway line. He showed me on his map."

"Let's go and have a look at this map, shall we?"

They both walked to the front of HQ and studied the different coloured pins on the large diagram. The line of red pins was impressive; it stretched a quarter of the way from Heath in one direction and a quarter from Downsend in the other. Mason studied the key.

"No wonder the Police Commissioner was complaining," he remarked. "These represent the number of houses that have suffered a forced entry due to the occupants being unavailable at the time of the search."

"Must have upset a few potential witnesses," Willis mused. "As well as costing a lot in compensation, of course."

"Quite. I think I'm going to have to put a stop to it."

At that point his mobile phone rang. "Excuse me a moment." Mason wandered off a short distance from Willis.

"Mason here," he answered.

"Good morning sir, it's Metropolitan Police Dog Unit control room here, Inspector Neave speaking. Sorry to trouble you, but we've been unable to contact Mr Bennett."

"No, that's not a problem, please continue."

"I've just had a report from one of our units, and the dogs have tracked the Professor's scent to a caravan located about half a mile away from Monty's fields. Apparently they were acting consistently with a find."

"Great work! Any sign of the Professor, or anyone else?"

"Not in person, but officers did find a strip of red material hanging from a side window, as if somebody had attempted to climb through it."

"Red material! Such as we found on the fence?"

"It would appear so. We have sent it off to be analysed. Also, we searched the inside of the caravan and there were signs of recent activity such as food wrappers in the bin and tea bags, etc. The dogs indicated that the Professor had been in the rear bedroom."

"This may be difficult to answer, but do you know when we will have the forensic results?"

"Two or three hours maximum, sir."

"Marvellous! That really would be helpful. Do we know who owns the caravan?"

"We are trying to contact the landowner now, sir. As soon as I have confirmation I will relay back to you."

"Thank you, Inspector. Please call me directly, if you would."

"Yes sir, will do."

As Mason ended the call he noticed that Willis was also on his phone. He waited discreetly for him to finish before striding back over.

"I've just had some interesting news. The dog unit have found a caravan where they suspect the Professor has been held."

"Really? At last we seem to be getting somewhere. That was one of my sergeants on the phone and she confirmed that the witnesses have given a positive identification on the two men sitting on the train in front of the Professor."

"Wonderful! Who are they?"

"Two men who worked on the railway, sir."

"Please call me Peter, Simon. Now then, what are you planning to do next?"

"We could bring them in for questioning, or we could continue to have them surveilled. Craig has already organised it."

"You mean he knew about the potential suspects yesterday?"

"Yes. The witnesses had already pointed them out from a photograph, but we took them to the railway today for an ID in person."

Mason shook his head. "I was unaware of any of this. I don't suppose they have identified the train driver, Mr Sutton?"

"No, but they recognised the guard on duty that day. He gave us the wrong description of the suspects, so we think he was also involved."

"Right. So now we've got an ID on all of the suspects, do we not?"

Willis inspected his notes.

"All except for the mystery farmer, who we believe to be a Derek Barton. He was picked out by several witnesses on the photograph but he's not expected at work until this afternoon. I believe he is being followed, though."

Mason looked round the room and called over one of his staff from the Logistics area.

"Do we know who Craig had tasked with surveilling the suspects?"

"No, but I think it's on the whiteboard." He indicated to an easel next to Craig's desk.

"Oh yes, thanks very much. Here were are – Derek Barton, assigned to agents 36 and 37. You wouldn't know who they were, would you?"

The man looked at the desks, which were all displaying names with numbers next to them.

"Joe and Brandon," he replied.

"And would you have their mobile numbers – sorry, what is your name?"

"Matt Reeves, sir. I think I've got them stored on my phone. If not, Craig will have them."

"Craig's no longer working on this assignment."

"Oh!" Matt looked flustered as he searched through his contact list.

"Yes, here we are, this is Joe's."

"Would you mind calling it for me?"

"Certainly." The young man rang the number but there was no reply. He shook his head.

"No answer?" Mason looked surprised. "What time is it now?"

"10.45, sir.

At that point Woody came rushing into the room to speak to Willis.

"Sir, I've got Romsey Police on the phone and they've just been called to an incident at the Military Canal."

"What's that, Woody? What kind of incident?"

"Two men have been found lying on the ground; apparently they've been attacked. I've got PC Goddard on the phone now."

"Can I speak to him?" demanded Mason. "MI8 here. Can you tell me what's happened?" Mason listened to the policeman for a while. "Is he able to speak? Okay, I'll pass him over to one of his colleagues. Matt, could you have a word with Joe first?"

Matt took over the phone. "Hello? Is that Joe? Hello?"

There was a pause.

"Are you okay, Joe? It's me, Matt. Is Brandon with you? Sorry, you're very faint." He pressed the phone to his ear. "Do you need an ambulance? Just a minute, I'll tell Mr Mason." Joe turned to speak to Mason, still with the phone to his ear. "Joe sounds very confused. He says they have both been attacked, and he can't find his phone. The

143

policeman brought him round, but Brandon is still semi-conscious."

"Can I speak to him?" Mason took the handset. "Hello, Mason here. Was it Barton who attacked you? I see." He softened his tone and slowed his voice. "And whereabouts in the park are you? By the river, next to the bridge. Okay, Joe. Is Brandon all right? Coming round, I see. Well listen, Joe, you are to stay there and wait for an ambulance. Do you understand? Yes? Okay, pass me back to the police constable." His voice became official again. "Can you get these men to hospital for a check-up? Is that the ambulance I can hear? Oh, good. We also need an all-ports alert issued for a Derek Barton – I'll give you to one of my colleagues for more details. Can you keep talking to the policeman, Matt, and provide him with the suspect's details?"

"Yes, sir." Matt took over the conversation.

Mason turned to speak to Willis. "It would seem Derek Barton has attacked our two men and gone on the run."

"Oh dear, that changes things a bit. They know that we are onto them now."

"Excuse me, Simon, I've got to have a word with the team." He strode to the centre of the hall. "Ahem, Gentlemen, may I have a word?"

The room immediately fell silent.

"I just wanted to update you all on the latest concerning the investigations. As some of you may know, I have taken back over the investigation with immediate effect. Craig will play no further part in it."

A murmur went round the room.

"We have located a caravan where it appears the Professor was taken, but he is no longer there. We don't know whether he managed to escape or is still being held captive."

More murmuring ensued, until Mason held his hand up.

"We have also identified five potential suspects, all of whom work on the railway. One of them has gone on the run after apparently attacking two of our team, who are currently receiving medical attention."

Shocked voices sounded again.

"I'm not an expert but I believe they are in no immediate danger. So what I would like us to concentrate on now are the five suspects we have identified. They are already being tailed, but one has escaped his followers. We obviously need people to focus on the hunt for this man – Derek Barton – any volunteers?"

A roomful of hands went up, colleagues anxious to find the man who had taken out their workmates. Mason picked the two nearest to him.

"Okay, the other men are already being watched, but I'd like forensic reports on telephone calls and bank statements on them all. DCI Willis here will provide the men's details. What we are looking for is clues as to where they may have taken the Professor – caravans, holiday homes, that kind of thing. And is Geoff still here?"

"Sir!" Geoff put up his hand.

"Can I have a word with you now? The rest of you please see DCI Willis and he will provide details of the suspects in question. Is everybody clear on what they are doing?"

"Yes, sir!" came the response.

Mason walked over to the Communications area. "Right, Geoff, I've been questioning Dr Wells and he has provided me with the name of the person who he sent his text message to. Have you managed to have this phone verified?"

"Yes, we have traced bank statements for a top-up to this number belonging to a Mrs Doreen Wells."

"Okay. That is what he's told me; that's his mother. I think we no longer need to worry about Dr Wells, for the time being."

"Right, sir. Maybe I can help with one of the other suspects?"

"Yes, Geoff, that seems to be your area of expertise, so it would be most useful. Okay, can I leave you to speak to DCI Willis?"

"Yes, sir."

Satisfied that everything was now moving in the right direction, Mason went back to his office. He wanted to check the RHLR website and look at the locomotives in question. The *Green Dawn* was a beautiful engine, naturally enough in green. The *Southern Maiden* was a slightly duller shade of green, and looked smaller. He walked back to Dr Wells' office, which was still being guarded.

One man unlocked the door and they both stood aside to let Mason through. Dr Wells looked up with a hopeful expression in his eyes.

"We've managed to confirm the text message was sent to your mother, Dr Wells. So as far as I'm concerned, you are no longer under suspicion."

"Oh, thank you, Peter." Dr Wells stood up to leave.

"Just one thing – you are certain that you saw the *Green Dawn* that day? It couldn't have been another train – the *Southern Maiden*, for example? They are both green."

Dr Wells considered for a moment.

"No, I'm absolutely sure. I had my train driving lesson on the *Green Dawn*, and it was her that I saw that day, definitely."

"Okay, well that answers the question. Thank you very much. Have a good evening."

Dr Wells shook his hand. "I'm so sorry for putting Mark in danger. Please keep me informed if you find him."

"I will. Now go home and put your family's minds at rest. Good afternoon."

"Good afternoon," he replied, before rushing out of the door.

During the rest of the day further information continued to coming to light. The red material found at the caravan was a match for that on the wire. The caravan was owned by Derek Barton. Forensics on the bank accounts of Alan Rochester and Roy King showed that Alan owned a boat which he kept on Downsend foreshore and Roy was a member of the RSPB, which had a reserve on Downsend. He kept Willis updated as each new piece of information arose.

"I'm getting the dog units to focus their search on the beachline and the bird reserve," he advised. "Both men know the area well and they could be hiding the Professor in a boat or a hideout somewhere."

"Good idea," Willis replied. "But have you seen the papers this morning? They seem convinced that the Professor is a Soviet spy. That doesn't make it easy for him to come forward, even if he has escaped."

"It's the PM's instructions. Until he is located we have to give good reason to apply for the search warrants and questioning of foreign aides. And personally speaking I don't think he wants to look silly making all this fuss if the Professor has been kidnapped by some locals with a grudge."

"I see. I thought there had to be a reason. Thank you for telling me." Willis paused. "Is there anything else about the case that you're not telling me? Because I get the feeling I'm being kept in the dark – all this fuss over one person; the ransom; and all the stuff in the papers when we know he's been kidnapped..."

"Forgive me Simon, you are right. But strict orders from the top mean that I'm not at liberty to tell you."

"I see."

"Let's just say, between you and I, that when we find the Professor I hope he still has his briefcase with him."

"Ah, I see – secret squirrel stuff – we're really looking for two things?"

"That's right."

Mason's mobile rang and he excused himself. It was the Aerial Support Unit. Only one source of heat had been detected within Len Sutton's house. The two watchmen confirmed he had not been seen to leave the building all day. Mason sighed. He was beginning to wonder if the Professor was still alive. Where they were hiding him was still a complete mystery.

Now to sort out the Spanish Inquisition along the railway track. No time to rush back home and see Becky tonight. He would have to give her a call and apologise.

CHAPTER TWENTY-THREE
Homecoming

THERE wasn't much time for goodbyes on Monday; the Professor was too busy getting ready for his big escape to Downsend Power Station. Len had got up at six and cooked a special full English breakfast, which they both enjoyed in the Shed. Then they discussed what Mark should say and shouldn't say to the authorities, who were bound to ask a ton of questions about where he'd been and who he'd met over the past three days.

"I'll do my best to deny all knowledge of you," he told Len, in between crunching on toast.

"Thanks, Mark, that's more than I've a right to expect."

"I don't think it'll work – they are the security services, after all – but it might put them off for a few days. And that will give you time to clean this place up and get rid of any traces of me being here."

"Good point. As soon as you leave I'll get the bleach out."

"And I suggest burying my suitcase somewhere. Don't just put it out with the rubbish."

"Ah yes, thanks for that, I probably would have done that without thinking. Look at the time, Mark. Don't want to keep the train waiting."

Mark finished his tea and they both took the steps up to Len's kitchen, where he peered out into the darkness cautiously.

"Can't hear anything yet," he murmured, "I'll open the back door, but we'd better not start talking in case anyone hears us. I won't put the light on, either."

"Okay," Mark whispered. He held his briefcase close to him as they waited. The cold morning air came rushing in to the conservatory, causing their breath to show as puffs of steam.

Len put his hand behind his ear as a sign for Mark to listen. He nodded. In the distance could be heard the faint chugging of a steam train heading in their direction. It stopped right on cue at the rear of Len's gate. He went first, indicating that Mark should follow his footsteps on the path and not on the gravel. Len opened his back gate slowly, pulling the bolt across as quietly as he could.

Outside stood George in the driver's compartment of the *Dark Prince*. He indicated that the Professor should climb in the first carriage and kneel down, where there was a rug which Len pulled over him. Then he slid the door to and gave George the thumbs up. It was all done very smoothly, the train barely having stopped more than two minutes. Without looking back he released the brakes and set the train in motion.

It would normally take half an hour for the train to travel from Romsey Sands to Downsend Station, but this time it stopped a short distance away on Downsend Road. George dismounted the train and slid open the door closest to Gary's van, and tapped on Mark's back before uncovering the blanket.

The Professor was still holding his briefcase tightly. He climbed backwards out of the carriage and crouched down before moving as quickly as he could towards the back of a white van which had its rear doors open. He climbed in and a young man pulled the door shut behind him. It was a tight squeeze in-between the boxes of plastic cups on one side and the freezer unit on the other. The young man then got into the driver's seat and drove off slowly.

"Are you all right in the back there?" he called out.

"Yes, fine," Mark called back. They drove in silence for a while before Gary started talking.

"We'll be there in a few minutes," he said. "Remember to tell them that you were lost on Romsey Marsh and you flagged me down."

"Yes, I'm just a hitch-hiker," he replied. "So I suppose you'll be claiming the reward for bringing me in?"

Gary laughed. "That's the general idea."

"So what will you do with the money, may I ask?"

"If I get it, it would be like winning the lottery. My missus and I can buy some IVF treatment."

"Oh, that's marvellous! Really, I hope it works out for you. At least some good may come of all this."

"Thanks. I hope they've been treating you well. I see you've got a bump on your head."

It was the Professor's turn to laugh. "Well, that's another story. Obviously I objected to being taken as a prisoner, but thankfully they've seen sense.

"Right, we'd better stop talking. We're coming up to the entrance now."

"Okay."

The Professor's heart was in his mouth as the van went through security on the main gate. It was quite a drive to the car parking area before Gary stopped the van.

"Right," he said quietly, "I've parked as near as I can to the side exit close to the canteen."

Gary got out of the van and opened up the back door, before signalling for Mark to exit. Then he gave him a box to carry with one arm, with him holding fast to his briefcase in the other. It did look a bit odd, but they still had to go through Security.

"Right, are you ready?"

"As I'll ever be."

"Come on then." Gary led the way to the Security office, which was manned by two armed soldiers. "Here's my pass," he said, flashing it to them as he went through. Mark tried to follow, but was stopped.

"Pass?" asked the Guard.

"He's helping me out today," said Gary.

"No pass, no entry," said the soldier.

The Professor looked him squarely in the eyes. "I'm the missing Professor."

The two soldiers locked eyes, unsure what to do next. "Let's take him through to HQ," said the one on the left.

"I want to claim the reward," said Gary, following them as they marched the Professor through the side entrance.

"P*** off!" said the second soldier, indicating that he should stay where he was.

Gary watched as they took the Professor into the main HQ, feeling extremely sorry for him. They marched him directly up to Woody, who was the man in charge as Mason and Willis were both still in their hotel rooms. There was suddenly a great commotion as the night workers realised what had happened.

"Please get me out of here," begged the Professor.

"Okay, don't worry," said Woody. "Listen everyone, can you please calm down. The Professor's been through a terrible ordeal and he'd like some privacy."

The noise subdued somewhat. Woody led the Professor to the canteen area, with Gary following behind.

"What do you want to drink?" asked Woody

"Black coffee, two sugars, please."

Gary, who was listening, put his key into the machine and pressed the right buttons. "Here you are." He passed the cup to the Professor. "What would you like?" he asked Woody.

"Drinking chocolate, please," he replied gratefully. He turned back to the Professor. "I can't believe you're here. And this is the man who brought you in, is that correct?"

"Yes, he kindly stopped for me. I didn't know where I was and I flagged him down."

"I see. Well, would you like to come into my boss's office where we can talk more privately?"

"Yes, that's a good idea. I'll bring my coffee with me, if I may?"

"Of course. Right, well – what's your name?" he asked the man who had given him his drink.

"Gary."

"Gary, thanks very much."

"I'd like to apply for the reward."

"Oh, I see. Well, that's not really my department. I tell you what, you work here, don't you?"

"Yes, filling the vending machines."

Woody got out his notebook. "Write your details down in here and I'll pass them on to the person concerned – name, address and phone numbers. Is that okay?"

"It'll have to be, I suppose." Gary reluctantly gave his details and Woody returned the notebook to his pocket.

"Right, let's go," he said, leading the way to Mason's office. It was empty as Mason had worked until midnight the day before. Woody sat in the Chief's chair and indicated Mark should sit on the plastic chair the other side.

"My name is DS Dunwoody – please call me Woody, everyone else does. I just want to make a few brief notes, Professor Hills, and then I'll call my boss. Is that okay?"

"Of course, but I doubt I can tell you much."

"The good news is that you look well and I see you still have your briefcase. Does it contain what I think it does?"

"Oh yes, all the plans are here. The kidnappers weren't interested in them."

"Really? Well, that's extremely fortunate. Did they not even look in there?"

"No – well, yes, they searched it for a mobile phone. I told them the diagrams were for a presentation and they left them alone."

"I see. And how many kidnappers were there?"

"Four or five, I'm not sure. They were wearing masks."

"What, all the time?"

"Yes."

"What about when they kidnapped you?"

"Ah. Well not then, obviously, but I don't remember much about that." He felt the bump on his head. "I can remember the man who attacked me, though. He was tall, dark and built like a heavyweight boxer."

"Well, that's something. Just a minute, I'll go and get some photos. Won't be long."

"Would it be all right if I called my family to let them know I'm okay?" The Professor pointed to the phone on the desk. "Only I don't know where my mobile is."

"Of course. Sorry, I should have thought of that first, please go ahead. As for your mobile, I might have some news on that. I'll be back shortly."

As Woody went outside, Mark heard him call over two of Mason's men and ask them to guard his room and make sure that nobody went in or came out of it. Feeling slightly claustrophobic again, he took two puffs on his inhaler before calling both sons. They were both so thrilled to hear from him that it brought tears to his eyes. They said they were coming to see him right away. He asked them to let his ex-wife, Alison, know too, although he wasn't so sure what her reaction would be.

Woody returned with Geoff, who was bearing the Professor's mobile in a plastic evidence bag. Mark stood up as they came into the office.

"Professor Hills? Very glad to see you!" Geoff exclaimed. The men shook hands. "Are you okay?"

"A bit tired, but other than that, yes."

"I'm Geoff, and I've been working on the case. Do you recognise this phone?" He handed over the sealed bag.

"It certainly looks like mine. Where did you find it?"

"I believe in a field somewhere, by the railway line."

"It must have fallen out of my jacket pocket. Such a shame I didn't have it earlier. Can I keep it now?"

"I'm not sure if we've finished with it yet, sir."

"Oh well, you'd better have it back." He handed it over reluctantly.

"Thanks very much, sir. I'll pass you back to DS Dunwoody, then, and let everyone else know you're back."

The Professor groaned. "I suppose you have to?"

"Geoff, perhaps you could hold off for now and just let Mr Mason know?"

"If that's what you'd prefer, I'll be very discreet. Goodbye for now."

Woody waited for him to leave and closed the door behind him.

"Just for my benefit, Professor, can you tell me what your relationship was like with Dr Wells?"

"Ray Wells? He's one of my oldest friends. Is he here?" the Professor sounded excited.

"I'm afraid not, but we'll let him know that you're okay."

"Thanks. I expect he's been worried sick, as have my family. My sons are on their way to see me, by the way."

"That's fine. Now, are you hungry, or is there anything else you need?"

"I'd love a shower and a change of clothes. Do you think you could arrange that?"

"Certainly! I'll get somebody to go to your house and bring some things over. There's also a shower block here. Now, I know you probably just want to go home but first we would like you to be examined by a doctor. And I know you will be interviewed more formally and asked to make a statement."

The Professor sighed. "I'd really like to hand over these diagrams to Dr Wells personally. I don't want anyone else to get their hands on them. Can I speak to him, please?"

"Of course. But first I'd appreciate it if you could look at this photograph we have of potential suspects. The information we have is that it was carried out by railway staff. Did you realise that?"

"No, not at all. Why would they do that?"

"We can only speculate at the moment. Now, do you recognise any of the people in this photo?" Woody spread the Christmas photograph in front of him.

"Ah! That may be the chap who knocked me out." He pointed to Derek.

"Okay, that is one of the leads we are following already. What about the others?"

"Mm, no, I couldn't say for certain. Possibly one or two look familiar, but I wouldn't like to say for certain. I only saw them briefly before the kidnapping."

"So they kidnapped you, what happened next, Professor?"

He took a sip of coffee. "I was unconscious, and when I awoke I was in an old caravan. I tried to escape but they stopped me. Then I think they drugged my drink, because the next thing I remember I was in a dark hole underground."

"Really? What sort of hole?"

"Possibly an old tunnel. It was very dirty and it was difficult to tell what it was used for. But it was definitely underground. And one of the kidnappers was put in charge of me. As I said, I never knew who he was because they all wore face masks – Guy Fawkes masks. They chained me to an old pipe while I was unconscious, with a chain round my ankle, and when I woke I was laying on an old sofa. That's pretty much where I stayed until they let me go."

"And that was this morning?"

"Yes, that's right. They said they were letting me go because I was more trouble than I was worth. Then they blindfolded me, tied my hands behind my back with cord and led me out of the tunnel. I was driven around for about five minutes when they opened the back of the van and pulled me out, cut the cord and blindfold and drove off again. They were still wearing masks. I could see the power station in the distance so I just started walking in that direction. Luckily, that young man drove past and said he was heading my way."

"That was Gary?"

"Yes, that's right."

"And you'd never seen him before?"

"No, he wasn't one of the kidnappers, I'm sure."

"How can you be certain?"

"They weren't young men that kidnapped me, I could tell by their voices and their physique. Even the man who attacked me wasn't young, I'm sure of that."

"It sounds quite an ordeal, Professor. I can assure you that we are going to deal with your kidnappers very severely indeed. We already think we know who they are."

"Right. That's good, yes. Now, can I speak to Dr Wells please?"

Woody searched for Dr Wells' phone number and dialled it on the landline before passing it over to him.

"Ray, it's me!"

"Good god, where are you?

"It's all right, I'm here, in one of your offices." Both men started laughing.

"I'm so relieved, we've all been really worried about you."

"I've been worried myself! But I'm hoping you can come in and I can hand you these diagrams personally. I don't want to give them to anyone else. What you do with them after that is up to you."

Dr Wells hesitated. "Well, I wasn't planning to come in today. It's a bit complicated – but all right then, seeing as it's you! Give me an hour and I'll be there."

"Great. I'm in a little room by the canteen, with one of the police officers."

"Can I speak to him?" asked Woody, taking the handset. "I was going to suggest to Professor Hills that he have a shower and get changed, and he could have a lie down in the Sick Bay."

Professor Hills interrupted. "Oh no, I'm not going anywhere until I've handed these plans over. I want to sit here until Ray arrives."

"Did you hear that, Dr Wells? He's here in Mr Mason's office, waiting for you. Okay, see you shortly."

CHAPTER TWENTY-FOUR
Mason & Willis combine forces

PETER MASON sat opposite Simon Willis in his tiny office. Both looked the worse for wear, having got up and dressed hurriedly on hearing the news of the Professor's reappearance.

"The problem is, Simon, that I can't possibly tell the PM that Professor Hills has suddenly appeared, Houdini-like, outside the power station. What does that say about our national security?"

"Hmm yes, I admit that doesn't sound too good. They are going to need to have a security review, at the very least."

"Yes, of course. But I'm at a loss what to tell him."

Willis pondered. "Why not say, somebody found him wandering in the road and they brought him here, where he made himself known on arrival? That's what happened, isn't it? You don't have to mention about him getting past all the roadblocks."

"Yes, that does sound better. Of course, somebody is going to get a bullet up their backside over this lapse in security. And another thing, I've had the doctor's preliminary findings, and the Professor's urine sample shows that he has consumed a large amount of alcohol. In fact, he's over the legal limit."

"Very hospitable kidnappers then?"

"Indeed! I also get the feeling that he's protecting them, to some extent. And that worries me. Have you ever had experience of this type of thing?"

"Not exactly. We've had hostage–type situations where a distraught father kidnaps his children, that kind of thing. And domestic violence, of course, where the wife refuses to testify."

"Hmm. I think we are seeing a case here of 'Stockholm syndrome' or 'capture bonding'.

"Possibly, yes. Do we know yet where they kept him?"

"No. Do you think that it's relevant?"

"Well, I'm not sure. I suppose if they looked after him, kept him fed and watered – including alcohol, by the sounds of it – and weren't unnecessarily cruel – maybe he empathised with their cause?"

"Yes, good point. We definitely need to discover where he was kept. I'm thinking of rounding up all the people we suspect of being involved in the kidnapping and questioning them separately, now that he's turned up."

"What about the one who got away?"

"Yes, our prime suspect, Derek Barton. Quite a few possible sightings, as far afield as Scotland, England and Wales. We are checking them all out, but it's a huge task."

"If there's anything we can do to help...?"

"Thank you, Simon, yes, perhaps if you assisted with the local sightings that would be a great help."

"I'll see to it right away. What about the person who brought him in, I heard they were claiming the million pounds reward?"

"A Mr Gary Stiles. We've done a check on him and can you believe that he is the son-in-law of George Cuthbert, the station master."

"Aah! Well, that's pretty conclusive. They were all involved somehow, then. He didn't just happen to drive past and find the Professor wandering up the road."

"Quite! And if he thinks we're going to pay him a million pounds then he's going to be sadly disappointed."

Willis raised his eyebrows. "I didn't know WE were going to be paying it. I thought it was raised by friends and colleagues?"

"Let's just say it's been officially sanctioned."

"Right. Well I'll keep schtum on that. But I think it would be a good idea to make a move now, before they manage to cover their tracks, so to speak."

They both laughed at the unintended pun.

"Yes, I'll make my call to the PM and then arrange for them all to be brought in for questioning. Thanks very much for your help, Simon, you've made things a lot clearer in my mind."

"No problem. I'll keep you informed if anything new develops.

"Me too. I'll update you later on, in any case."

"Thanks."

Willis left Mason to his difficult phone call, shutting the door behind him.

CHAPTER TWENTY-FIVE

Interviews

INTERVIEWING the suspects was not going very well. They had all agreed that they were involved, and all claimed that it was a joint venture, with no Ringleader. Mason had been horrified to discover that Len Sutton's home had backed onto the railway line, with a convenient gate at the bottom of the garden, but nobody had been watching the rear of his house. It occurred to Mason that the Professor could have been moved up and down the line with ease, but this still did not solve the mystery of where he had been kept. A couple of the suspects, when questioned, had said that the Professor had been held in a shed, but had resolutely refused to give more details.

"Is it underground?" Mason asked Len.

"No comment."

"Is it a train shed?"

"No comment."

"Why did the Professor have alcohol in his system? Did you try to drug him with alcohol?"

"No comment."

And so it went with the other interviews, mostly "no comment" answers.

Willis, who had sat in on the interview, discussed the progress at lunch with Mason. The two were becoming trusted friends.

"How was the PM?" Willis asked.

"He was very congratulatory, thank goodness," Mason replied. "He didn't want to know all the details. His words were, 'whatever it took, thank you'."

"I see." Willis ate the rubbery cheese sandwich offering from the vending machine thoughtfully. "What did he say about the reward?"

"I didn't get a chance to mention it."

"And how is the Professor?"

"He's been reunited with his sons, and given his diagrams over to Dr Wells, so we've released him to go home. We're hoping to speak to him tomorrow, when he's had a proper night's sleep."

"No doubt he's exhausted. It must have been a terrifying few days," Willis remarked. "Now, where on *earth* did they keep him?"

Woody joined the pair at lunch and said that he had an interesting conversation on tape from a woman who had rung Crimestoppers with some information. After they had eaten they went back to Mason's office to hear it.

"Actually, something unusual did happen last Friday." The woman's voice sounded hesitant. *"It's probably nothing, but – "*

"What day would that be, Madam?"

"Let me see – 26 September. I don't want to get anybody at the railway in trouble, you know, they all work so hard and a lot of it is unpaid, and I know they're not supposed to run the trains late in the evening."

"Anything to do with the railway is obviously very important to our inquiries at the moment, madam."

"I see. Yes, of course it must be. Well, last Friday night, it was about half past ten at night when I heard the locomotive going past."

"At 10.30. Was this unusual?"

"Very, I've never heard it so late. They do have occasional evening events, but never at that time in the evening. It's all the traffic, you see, at the crossroads. There's been some terrible accidents in the past in broad daylight."

"Yes, I'm aware of them."

"I thought I must be hearing things, so I actually opened my back door and stood on the patio, and although I couldn't see it, sure enough one of locomotives was going past. There wasn't any steam so it must have been one of the diesel ones."

"I see. So you thought it was strange at the time?"

"Very strange, because it stopped before the station. And it didn't sound its horn before it went over the level crossing down the line at Romsey Sands, and that's where the accidents are likely to happen."

"What happened next, madam?"

"Well, it waited a little while – maybe five minutes – and then it went back up the line. That's all I noticed, anyway."

"Thank you very much indeed, madam, you've been very helpful. If you notice anything else, please call us again immediately on this number."

"I will," she said.

"I bet that's when they moved the Professor from the caravan," remarked Willis.

"Yes, Friday – that sounds about right. And she said they stopped before it got to the station at Romsey Sands – is that near to where Mr Sutton lives, by any chance?"

"Yes!" exclaimed Willis. "That's exactly where he lives, a few doors down from Romsey Sands Station. His house had already been searched so they thought it was safe to keep him there."

Woody looked unsure. "But I thought you had agents peering in through his windows and helicopters flying overhead?"

"So I believe, Woody. But we had nobody watching the back of Mr Sutton's house," Mason explained.

"So do we think he was kept in the garden? In a tent, or such-like?" queried Willis.

"No, I'm sure the helicopter would have spotted that," replied Mason.

"It really is a mystery," Willis said for the umpteenth time.

It was Sergeant Janice Goldsmith who finally cracked the conundrum. She had printed off some newspaper articles, which Willis found on his desk.

"What's this, Janice?"

"Sir, I was reading up on the internet about Downsend and Romsey Sands, and I came across this article about the area during the war."

"*'Pipe Line Under The Ocean'* – what's this?"

"The PLUTO bungalows, sir. I was wondering whether this is Mr Sutton's bungalow."

Mason scan read the article and then studied the photograph of a white building with a flat roof.

"I haven't seen Sutton's bungalow, Janice, have you been there?"

"Yes sir. It's the same shape as in the photo."

"Right! Ask Woody to get the search teams in there, including the dog unit. I want the house and garden searched right away."

"Yes sir."

"And Janice – well done! If this proves to be correct, you'll be in for a commendation."

"Thank you, sir," she called out as she rushed away.

"Well, well," Willis mused to himself. "Good old detective work has prevailed. My plan to keep her on the road has paid dividends." He smiled. "I won't say anything to Simon just yet, in case it's a red herring."

Forty minutes later the confirmation came. They had discovered a trap door hidden in the conservatory and descended into the Shed. And although Len had made a good job of clearing up, it was pretty obvious from its marks that the broken pipe by the settee had been worn away by something metallic.

"Gotcha!" Willis exclaimed when he heard the news. He briefed Mason before they both entered the temporary interrogation room at the power station. After the usual preliminaries, Willis produced the newspaper article and placed it in front of Len.

"Mr Sutton, is this your bungalow?"

Len visibly whitened when he saw the faded black and white photograph.

"Please answer the question," Mason insisted.

"Yes."

"This is where you kept the Professor hidden, isn't it?" Willis asked.

Len hesitated. "Yes."

"Thank you! I'm glad we've cleared that up." He looked at Mason, who nodded for him to continue. "And you kept him chained up to a pipe in the corner, is that right?"

"Yes." Len looked ashamed. "In the beginning we did keep him as a prisoner, yes. But then we were too afraid to let him go."

"Too afraid of being caught, you mean!"

"No – well, that too, of course – but we kept hearing on the news and reading in the papers that he was wanted, dead or alive. They thought he was a Russian spy."

"Come now, Mr Sutton," Mason interjected, "if you were so worried you could have just opened your front door, walked outside and explained what had happened. Or did you think they were going to shoot you both?"

"I didn't know what to think," Len mumbled. "I knew there were special agents watching me out the front. I knew

166

there were helicopters flying overhead all the time. And I saw the armed soldiers..."

"The Professor has told us that you said he was more trouble than he was worth, bundled him into a van and dumped him in the middle of the road. That doesn't sound very caring, Len," said Willis.

"That's not true, he escaped! He locked me in the cellar and he could have run away, but saw the Sunday newspaper and was too scared."

"I don't believe you."

"It's true!" Len persisted. "He's probably just trying to put you off the scent. We smuggled him to Downsend on a train and then somebody took him by van to the station."

Willis and Mason looked at each other, remembering the *Crimestoppers* phone call.

"Why didn't you leave him at Downsend Station, he could have walked?" Mason asked.

"Same reason. We thought it would be safer if we took him right inside the power station, where his friends were."

"Who is 'we', Len?" asked Willis.

He paused. "Myself and the Professor."

"So the Professor went along with this plan?"

"Yes!"

Willis and Mason looked at each other.

"We're just going to have a chat outside, Mr Sutton. For the benefit of the tape, interview suspended at 12.30pm."

They went outside and closed the door.

"Do you think he's lying?" asked Mason.

"No, in a funny sort of way I believe he's telling us the truth. He's not telling us everything, of course."

"No, patently not. He hasn't mentioned the role of any other members of the gang." Mason checked his watch. "With any luck Professor Hills will be back here now, ready for his interview. I'm going to find out."

Willis nodded. "Okay. I'll get Woody to come back in with me and ask Len some more questions. They both walked towards HQ and found Woody heading towards them.

"I was coming to look for you, sir," he said to Willis. "The Professor seems very upset this morning."

"Do we know why?"

"I'm not sure. I mentioned that we had six people being questioned about his kidnapping, and he asked whether we had caught Derek yet. I told him 'no' and that's when he became upset."

"Not to worry, Woody, I'm going to see him now," said Mason, "whereabouts is he?"

"In the canteen, sir."

"And I'd like you to come back with me while I finish interviewing Mr Sutton," said Willis, turning back in the other direction.

Woody followed meekly behind.

CHAPTER TWENTY-SIX
The Professor Turns

PROFESSOR HILLS was indeed agitated. He had driven quite a distance from his home in south London, after an emotional reunion with his ex–wife and sons the previous evening. For the first time he had considered the possibility of retiring from work and spending more time with his family. At Downsend his arrival had coincided with one of the locomotives from the miniature railway, which had blown its horn as it went past. He was secretly pleased to see that the train was still running as normal. He had also suddenly felt hungry.

Woody had met the Professor at reception and steered him towards the canteen. Hills headed straight for the vending machine. It was empty. A horrible thought struck him.

"I wonder where the young chap is who brought me in?" he asked Woody.

"I believe he is being held for questioning."

"What? He was nothing to do with my kidnapping!"

"Well that's what they're looking into, Professor. There could be a link. We're holding six people at present."

"So have you found Derek?"

"No, I don't think so."

"Oh!" He started pacing the floor. "Is Peter Mason in? I'd like a word with him."

"Certainly sir, I'll go and find him."

A few minutes later, Mason appeared.

"Is everything all right, Professor Hills?"

"Not really. I'd like a word in private, if I may."

"Yes, of course. Come back to my office and we can have a chat. Shall I get us a tea or coffee to take back with us?"

"I don't believe the vending machine is working."

Mason stared at the long queue in the canteen. "I see. Not to worry, I'll get somebody to bring one to us." Mason led the way back to his cubicle office and sat down at the desk. "Now, what will you have?"

"Coffee, black with two sugars please."

Mason typed an email to one of his staff. The Professor sat down in the chair opposite him.

"Is something troubling you, Professor?"

"Mark – please call me Mark."

"Thank you. And I'm Peter."

"I believe you have rounded up the people you believe kidnapped me, is that correct?"

"That's right, Mark. I've been interviewing a Mr Sutton only a short while ago. His version of events differs considerably from the one you gave us yesterday."

"Mr Sutton being Len?"

"Yes, that's right." Mason paused. "Now, DCI Willis will deal with the formalities later, when he asks you for an official witness statement. But is there something which you'd like to discuss with me in private?"

The Professor nodded.

"Please, feel free to say whatever you like. There's no hidden tape recorders here, I can assure you."

"Right. Well, let's start with my invention, the Nuclear Waste Reprocessing System." He empathised the word 'my'.

"Yes, go on."

"I've been working on the NWRS for the last twenty years. Mostly, might I add, at my own expense. Let alone all the hours I've put into it, or the effect on my health."

"So I understand."

"I deliberately haven't patented it because I had no intention of making the idea commercially available. I was going to give the UK a head start."

"I see. Very decent of you."

"Thank you. But now, at the first sign of my disappearance, I see that I am being accused of being a Government Spy – what were those words in the papers – "Wanted – Dead or Alive!"

Mason went to speak, but Mark spoke over the top of him.

"I've never worked for the Government, so how can I be a government spy?"

"My apologies, Mark. We weren't in a position to confirm or deny the headlines for security reasons."

"Poppycock! What about my security? I could have been shot!"

"No, no, I can assure you that would not have happened."

"What about if a member of the public decided to take matters into their own hands? I'm sure there's many who would be happy to take a pot shot at me for a million pounds!"

Peter Mason shuffled uncomfortably. "So is that why you decided not to escape when the chance came?"

"I see Len's told you about that. You're damn right! I was eternally grateful when they came up with a plan to get me to the power station without being seen. And now, I hear, the young man who brought me here has been arrested!"

"That is correct. You do realise he's the son-in-law of the Station Master?"

"No, but I don't care about that. He told me he needed the reward to pay for some IVF treatment. I hope he's still getting that money?"

Peter Mason was silent for a few moments. "If that is your wish, Mark, I can certainly look into it."

"Thank you!" The Professor seemed to calm down. "So what's going to happen to the others?"

171

"That is a matter for the Police. They've committed a very serious crime and caused a great deal of trouble. There's no way they could be let off with a slap on the wrists. You do understand that, don't you?"

"They did it for something they loved – the Railway! And now I've had a few days to think about the important things in life, I realise that my family, friends and the things I love are more important than work or money."

"Very fine sentiments. I'm sure that will be taken into consideration when they go for sentencing."

The Professor stood up and began pacing back and forth like a caged tiger. "Now that I've handed over my plans to Dr Wells, I no longer want anything to do with the project. I plan to retire to the Isle of Wight."

"Very sad to hear that, Mark, but I do understand after everything you've been through."

"I can see I'm not making myself clear. I think you will find, if you speak to Ray, that he will not be able to proceed without my assistance."

Mason paused. "I see. And why should that be, exactly?"

"Because the plans do not show everything! There are a few things in the process that I was going to explain rather than draw. But if I am no longer working on the project, that will be left for others to discover."

"I see." Mason considered this. "Is there anything that might persuade you to change your mind?"

"Yes! I do not want the plant to be built at Downsend, for a start. There are too many holes in the subsoil, which could raise the potential for leaks."

"Are you referring to the place where they kept you?"

"Partly, yes. Apparently there are plenty more dug-outs of a similar nature; in fact I believe there are no longer records of them all."

"I see. So where would you suggest it be built, then?"

The Professor thought for a few seconds. "Sandpoint. That's not too far from the Isle of Wight; I could commute there."

"Sandpoint, right. And while we are speaking so frankly, is there anything else that troubles you?"

"Yes, there is. I'd like my captors to be treated leniently. Even the one who attacked me."

"Mr Derek Barton? You do realise that apart from attacking you, he knocked out two of our agents?"

"I did see those reports on television, yes. But he is suffering from post traumatic stress syndrome. A spell in prison would do him no good at all. In fact, the railway was helping to keep him sane."

"Mark, none of us are above the law, even you or I! I cannot promise to keep him out of prison when he is discovered."

"Fair enough. I'm asking for leniency, that's all. And for that young chap, Gary, to get his million pounds."

"Right!" Mason sounded annoyed. "Is that all?"

"Yes."

"And if those things could be achieved, you would consider working on the project?"

"Yes."

Mason rose from his seat. "I'm going to have a word with Dr Wells to see what he thinks. And then I'll speak with the PM."

There was a gentle knock at the door.

"Come in!" A young man nervously entered with two cups of coffee on a tray. "Thank you, David. Please put them on the desk, there's no room for a tray. Thanks very much. Stay here, Mark, and drink your coffee. I may be some while." Mason locked his computer and left the room, closing the door behind him.

The Professor sat back down and laughed nervously before taking a sip of coffee. He was definitely acting out of character; normally his emotions were kept under control. Blackmail was also a novelty. He hoped he had not overplayed his hand, and that an old friendship would count for something when the chips were down.

CHAPTER TWENTY-SEVEN
Dr Wells Makes Amends

DR WELLS was puzzled. He had gone through Mark's diagrams with a fine tooth comb, and spent the morning writing algebraic formulas on the whiteboard in his office. He could understand the process of extracting the thermonuclear elements from the radioactive material, which was a brilliant leap forward in current understanding. These then underwent a process of fusion in order to create electricity and by-products. That part was explained fully in the slides. What was not explained, however, was how these by-products were then rendered harmless. The actual conversion process – the most important part – remained a mystery to him. He was so engrossed that he failed to hear Peter Mason knocking on his door, before walking in.

"Good morning, sir, I'm pleased to see you back at work again."

"Oh! Yes, good morning, Peter, I was so excited by what Mark has designed here that I simply had to come into work today. I always knew he was a genius, and this proves it!"

Mason looked at the equations on the whiteboard and tried to make sense of them. "Is everything here that you need in order to try out the new process?"

"If I'm honest, no. I can get so far – say three–quarters of the way along, but then there appears to be something missing."

"Is it important?"

"The most important part, actually – how to neutralise the by-products so that they are no longer radioactive. The process of creating electricity is all here, which is a massive improvement on our current technique, but as far as I can tell, the by-products must still be radioactive – albeit significantly less so than before. I'll have to ask Mark to explain it."

"I've just spoken to Professor Wells this morning, and he has indicated to me that he may withdraw from the project."

"Oh no! That would be disastrous!"

"Would you not be able to continue without his help?"

"It would take much longer without his guidance. And as I've explained, there's the missing element which we don't know about."

Mason paused. "Would you be able to figure it out?"

"I don't know, if I'm honest. Probably, yes – but it could take another five years to do so."

"Five years!"

"Yes. Or at the earliest – say two years, if we worked on it 24 hours a day. You must realise this is a lifetime's work here."

"I see." Mason was deep in thought. "The reason I'm asking is, the Professor has refused to part with this information unless we meet certain conditions with regards to him continuing on the project, and I wanted to run these past you."

"Really? I'm astonished!"

"Firstly, he does not want the NWRS to be built at Downsend."

"What? I can't believe it! I can only guess that the kidnappers are blackmailing him somehow."

"I think there's something in what you say. However, he seemed most adamant. So I have to ask you how you would feel about transferring over to Sandpoint in the west country?"

"Let me have a think." Dr Wells rubbed his chin for a few moments. "If that's what Mark is asking for, it's the least I can do. It's a nice part of the world, why not! If that's the difference between having Mark working on the project or us stumbling around in the dark, that's a very small price to pay."

"Excellent! Thank you very much, Ray. The other things he has asked for will need the PM's consent, but at least I can give him that good news. Thanks for being so accommodating."

The Prime Minister was equally magnanimous. "If we let Mr Stiles have the reward but still give him a suspended sentence, that would lead people to believe that the money did not come from the government."

"Yes, I suppose that's true. I dislike the whole idea of people profiting by crime, however."

"Perhaps 'crime' is too strong a word here, Peter – perhaps we should say 'event'."

"When compared to the others' involvement, yes."

"And then there's all the unwanted publicity. Them all standing up in Court and saying they believed the Professor's life was in danger so they couldn't let him go. And then, by the sounds of it, Professor Hills agreeing with them."

"Yes, I'm afraid he's bonded somewhat with his captors."

"Any news on the missing member of the gang?"

"Derek Barton, no, not yet sir. It troubles me that he could be let off scot-free for knocking three people unconscious."

"An ex-soldier suffering from PTSD. Surely he deserves a sympathetic hearing?"

"Humph!" Mason sounded disgusted.

"May I suggest we look on the bright side here? Two years of experimentation on nuclear fusion with no guaranteed outcome would be hugely expensive. A million pounds would soon fade into insignificance."

"For the greater good, then?"

"Yes, indeed! A new source of power for the nation; just what the economy needs."

"I see. Very well, I'll let the Professor know that his demands will be met."

"In the circumstances, they appear quite reasonable. He could have sold his invention for many times more than that."

"Yes, I understand. Very well, I'll have a word with him now."

"Thank you, Peter. You have the whole Cabinet's gratitude, I can assure you."

"Thank you, sir." Mason hung up the phone. He couldn't believe it, he was having to put a positive spin on a kidnapping event. That was the word, 'event' – not 'crime'. He needed to calm down before speaking to the Professor again.

Mason wandered into the canteen and ordered a strong coffee. Perhaps the Professor had a point after all. The most important things in life were your family and friends, and the things you love. He sat down and called a number on his mobile.

"Becky, is that you?"

"Yes – oh, hello." She sounded surprised to hear from him.

"Becky, I've got a suggestion to make. You're studying in London and my apartment in Knightsbridge is empty most of the time. Instead of racking up your student loan on rent, why don't you move in and look after it for me?"

"Really?" Becky sounded keen. "Okay, thanks Dad! That would be great!"

Mason smiled to himself. It was the first time she had called him 'Dad' for years. She had even said, 'Love you,' before hanging up. For the first time in ages, Mason's heart gave a little flip.

CHAPTER TWENTY-EIGHT
Derek's Return

DEREK had travelled all day without incident. No policemen had boarded his train to St Pancras station. He'd then caught the fast train from Paddington to Cardiff Central, again with no incident. He then found a coach heading past Tolgarth, a small village on the edge of the Beacons, and one that he remembered fondly from his younger days, training as a squaddie.

After collecting his rucksack from the coach luggage hold, Derek headed into the village. He was pleased to see that nothing much had changed from how he remembered it, thirty-five years ago. Feeling hungry, he recalled his favourite pub at the time, *The Traveller's Rest*. It used to serve nice pub food; tasty and cheap. It wouldn't still be here after all this time, would it? The time was only six-thirty but the streets were already dark, the street lights on. Darkness and hunger made him bold.

Derek smiled as he saw the old familiar sign at the end of the high street, beckoning him towards it. He hovered outside the pub for a few moments, peering through the mullioned windows. There only appeared to be half a dozen people inside. Taking off his dark glasses he ventured in to the saloon bar. A real log fire roared in the fireplace; the heat hitting him in the face together with the smell of beer. Perfect!

The barmaid welcomed him with a friendly smile. "What will you have?" she asked in a lilting voice.

"I'm starving, are you still serving food?"

"No, I'm afraid not." She saw his disappointment. "But wait a moment, if you don't mind Sunday roast heated up in the microwave?"

"That sounds lovely!" he replied. He pulled his large rucksack from his shoulders and placed it on the floor.

She smiled at him and disappeared behind the bar for a few moments, returning with a plate of food covered with a plastic lid. She took the lid off and revealed a roast chicken dinner. "How does that look to you?"

"Yes, I could definitely eat it," he replied encouragingly, "I'd even eat it cold, just like that."

She laughed a musical laugh. "Oh no, don't be silly. It'll only take a few moments to warm up."

She placed it into the microwave behind the bar. "Now then, can I get you anything else?"

"A pint of Young's, please." Derek had acquired the taste for this beer during his stint at Chelsea Barracks. He was always pleased to see it available. He took a good look at the woman as she poured his pint. Late thirties, maybe early forties? She had a round face and body with a buxom chest, dark hair and blue eyes that twinkled in the bar lights. Quite a looker, actually.

"That'll be seven pounds with dinner, then," she said, placing the pint on a beer mat.

"Prices have gone up a bit since I was here last," he joked, handing over a ten pound note.

She handed over his change and watched as he put two pounds in the Help for Heroes tin on the bar and the remaining coin back in his wallet.

"Aah, an old soldier then, are we?" Her eyes met his and her gaze seemed to reach into his soul.

"Yes I am, how can you tell?"

"I've seen quite a few come back here, over the years. Trying to re-live their youth, or when they've got troubles."

Derek gasped. The woman seemed to be reading his mind. She took the plate of hot food from the microwave and placed in on a tray, together with a knife and fork in a serviette.

"Why don't you sit on a table by the fire?" she suggested, pointing to a comfortable looking table and chair. "I'll bring the beer over for you."

"Oh, thanks very much," he said gratefully, pulling his rucksack over his shoulder with one hand and carrying the tray with the other. He noted her hands as she picked up his tray and was pleased to see she was wearing no ring. "Steady, man," he told himself.

"Have you found yourself a place to stay?" she asked.

"No, not yet. I was thinking of camping."

"I see. Not so nice this time of year, and we had floods not far from here. I've got some rooms available for £20 a night, including breakfast."

"That sounds very reasonable." Derek made himself comfortable by the fireplace. "That's a full English?"

"With some Welsh lava bread," she laughed.

"How can I resist?" He stared at her, trying to decide if she was flirting with him or not. He couldn't be sure.

"Okay, that's settled then. When you've finished I'll show you up to your room. Payment in advance, mind."

"Very wise," he replied, giving her a wink. She giggled back. Definitely flirting, he thought to himself.

An hour later, Derek asked to see his room. It looked basic but comfortable, with tea and coffee making facilities and a tv to watch. He handed over a £20 note and she placed a key in his hand.

"If you need anything, just dial zero and ask for me, Bronwen," she told him. "And your name is?"

"Andy," he replied, his middle name being the only one he could think of as she looked up at him. Those eyes were like all-seeing lasers into his soul.

"What time would you like breakfast?"

"Is eight o'clock okay?"

"Yes, fine. Well, I hope you have a good sleep, then. See you tomorrow."

"Thank you. Goodnight, Bronwen." He didn't give her a wink this time; that would have been too sleazy. He unpacked a few pieces of clothing and made himself comfortable, before switching on the TV. Derek's mugshot was still being shown on the news, but he was pleased by how much difference a simple haircut had made to his appearance. If he didn't shave for a few days, he thought he'd be unrecognisable. At ten o'clock he showered and hit the hay.

Derek slept surprisingly well, but at six o'clock he jumped out of bed as usual and went through his normal routine, resisting the urge to shave. He looked outside at the weather and contemplated a run, but settled for extra press-ups. Switching on the tv again, he was pleased that his face was no longer peering back at him from the screen. "A few more days and I'll be yesterday's news," he thought happily.

At ten to eight, whistling cheerily to himself, he went downstairs into the bar from where delicious smells were wafting.

"Good morning!" he called out to the empty bar. Bronwen and two other people appeared from a door.

"Morning, Andy. Tea or coffee, my love?"

"Tea please." He admired how she looked even better slightly dishevelled in her white apron.

A young woman brought in a pot of tea and a man of similar age brought over some toast.

"Thank you," he said to them.

Bronwen soon brought over his breakfast; two of everything, cooked to perfection.

"That looks delicious, thanks very much."

She smiled. "I hope you slept well?"

"Yes thanks. It's so quiet here, I slept like a log."

"Oh good. So will you be leaving us this morning?"

"Ah, I was going to come to that. Would it be all right if I stayed tonight?"

182

She looked pleased. "Of course it will. You can stay all week if you like."

He laughed. "We'll see. I'm pleased to see you've got some help."

"That's my daughter, Rowan, and her boyfriend. I couldn't manage this place without them."

"I'm going for a walk in the Beacons today," he told her, as she placed salt and pepper on his table.

"Oh, okay. Shall I make you a packed lunch?"

"Yes, that would be great."

"Do you have a flask? If not you can use one of mine."

"Thanks again. A hot drink would be good on a day like today. You're spoiling me now."

"And don't forget your mobile phone, in case you get lost."

"Ah. I haven't actually got one."

"No? Well, you can't go wandering off on your own without one, it's too dangerous."

He was touched by her concern. "Where would I get a phone round here?"

"Go to Jenkins Stores down the high street. They'll be open at nine."

"Thanks, Bronwen."

"No problem. Well I'll leave you alone now before your breakfast gets cold."

Derek tucked into his hearty breakfast, enjoying every mouthful. When he took his plates back to the bar, Bronwen handed over a packet of wrapped sandwiches, an apple and a flask of hot tea. "Don't forget the phone, mind," she told him, handing him a card with the Traveller's Rest telephone number on it.

"I won't. Thanks very much. I probably won't be back until late, so don't worry unduly."

Mobile purchased, he sauntered up the road and a plan began to form in Derek's mind. He was going to retrace his steps as a young soldier and visit some of the hills he had climbed many years ago. On he walked for about an hour, gradually recognising more and more of the landscape until he came upon Wootton Tor, as he'd known it.

"This is it!" he exclaimed aloud. Derek peered up to the top of the hill, shrouded in mist. Derek thought back to when he was a young soldier, doing his body fitness test. He'd had to run to the top of the hill and back again within an hour. He thought back wistfully to three of his friends who had been in the same Regiment who had died over the years. Colin, shot in Northern Ireland during the Troubles. Murray, blown up when he'd stepped on a landmine in Bosnia. Derek had been a few feet away when that happened, and still had nightmares about it. Then poor Justin, who had also witnessed the incident and committed suicide on his return home. He thought back to that day many years ago when the four of them had run up Wootton Tor together. He was the only one left now.

"I'm going to run up there one last time," he thought to himself. Starting at a slow jog he began to climb the hillside. It took him 45 minutes to reach the top, his lungs burning inside. He took off his rucksack and sat down, feet hanging over the edge of a rock. The view was spectacular for miles around, although the clouds hung so low in places he could almost touch them. Derek looked down. It would be so easy to jump now, and join his friends. All his troubles would be over, he wouldn't have to worry about going to prison or paying the bills any more. It was tempting, but something held him back. He could feel their disapproval. His brothers in arms, they didn't want him to do it. They wanted him to live on, for their sake.

Derek sat there for an hour or more remembering back to the old days, eating his lunch and drinking tea from his flask.

"Well boys, I'd better be getting back," he said out loud, before packing his rucksack again. "Thanks for your company."

He walked back down the other side of the tor, watching his step, thinking on what to do in the future. He felt ready to move on with his life now; take a new direction. Maybe Bronwen was the key, he thought to himself. Sounded like she needed a man around the place.

By the time he arrived back at the Travellers Rest it was just after four and starting to get dark. Bronwen's face lit up when she saw him walk through the door.

"Back safe and sound," he said to her, walking towards the bar. He saw her blush.

"Another pint?" she asked.

"Why not? Think I deserve one after all that walking."

He looked around the place, where a few people were sitting chatting and an old man was reading a newspaper. He noticed another newspaper on one of the tables, so took his beer over there to have a read.

"Professor Hills found!" screamed the headline. He read on anxiously. Six people had been arrested – no names given. Six! Len, Henry, Alan, Roy and himself only made five, where had the extra two people come from? The article didn't say. The Professor had been found under mysterious circumstances, of which the police were refusing to give details. And somebody had claimed the million pounds reward. Traitor! Who had done that, he wondered?

Derek was so busy reading that he never noticed Bronwen standing beside him.

"Sorry," he said, startled to see her there.

"Would you like any tea tonight?"

"Oh, yes please. Can I have it in my room, though?"

Bronwen seemed a little put out. "Oh right. Well, I don't see why not. Is lamb stew okay?"

"That sounds delicious. Er, I think I'd better settle up with you, too. I'm moving on tomorrow."

Now he could tell she was disappointed.

"Is everything all right?" she asked.

"Yes, everything's fine. Something's just come up and I've got to go back home."

"Oh, I see. Well, sorry to hear that, Andy. I was going to offer you a job as a barman if you wanted to stay."

"Really?" Derek was suddenly in two minds whether to go back or not. "I tell you what, if I manage to sort things out I might take you up on it, okay?"

Bronwen nodded and gave a sad smile. He could see she didn't believe him, although he was serious enough. But right now he had other things to worry about. Two people had been arrested who were innocent, and he had to go back and make things right. He downed the beer and took his rucksack up to his room, where he made a call to the railway station.

"Hello?" answered a young woman, whose voice he recognised.

"Hi Jenny, it's Derek."

"Oh!" she gasped. "Everyone's been looking for you. We've been really worried."

"Really?" he laughed. "Can you tell me what's going on? I've read something in the newspapers."

"Well, George has been arrested. I'm the only one here in the office."

"George? What's George done?"

"Something to do with the missing Professor, I think.

"He had nothing to do with it!"

"How do you know?" she asked.

"Never you mind," he replied. "So who else has been arrested, then? It says six people in my paper."

"George's son-in-law, Gary; Henry, Len, Alan and Roy." She paused. "Is that why you ran away?"

"Yes."

"Oh no!"

"But don't worry, I'm coming back tomorrow to sort it out. It was nothing to do with George, and I'll tell them that."

"But they'll arrest you, too. Maybe you should stay where you are."

"Thanks for worrying about me, sweetheart, but my mind's made up. I'm not running away from anything any more. And I'll get George's son-in-law out of trouble. It was nothing to do with him, either."

"That's good of you Derek. Be careful, then," she warned.

"I will," he replied, before hanging up.

He smiled to himself. It was good the hear that people were genuinely worried about him. That was a nice surprise. Mind made up, he began packing his things for the morning. There was a light knock on the door, which he opened. To his surprise it was Rowan, who delivered his dinner.

"Thanks very much, that smells delicious! Oh, wait a minute, here's your mum's flask back."

The girl took it from him and smiled. "Thanks," she said.

"And can you tell your mum how much I've enjoyed these past few days, and that I'll be back as soon as I can."

Rowan smiled again. "Okay, I'll tell her."

Derek closed the door and smiled to himself. There was no doubt about it, Bronwen was a cracking cook. If he didn't get locked up for years then he'd make his way back here as soon as he could.

CHAPTER TWENTY-NINE
The Final Verdict

AT FOUR on Tuesday afternoon, Peter Mason stood at the front of HQ and asked for silence.

"As of five p.m. today, HQ is being closed down," he announced. A buzz of excitement went round the room. "You may have heard that we have located the missing suspect, who has given us a very full statement of events from the beginning of the incident until now. As a result of this new information, we have been able to release all the suspects on bail pending their appearance in Court next week."

A murmur of surprise went round the hall. Mason held his hand up for silence.

"Professor Hills is safe and well and our two men are out of hospital and recovering at home, which is a good result all round."

"Hear, hear," said DCI Willis, standing nearby."

"I wanted to thank each and every one of you for your sterling efforts in getting this case resolved so quickly. You have all played your part in accomplishing this, so it may seem perverse to single anybody out for their individual actions, when so much has been achieved by teamwork. However, there were two very significant key pieces of information that ultimately led to the solving of this case, so DCI Willis and I would like to congratulate those two individuals who have thought outside of the box, so to speak. Would you like to go first, Simon?"

"Yes, indeed. For me, the officer who has performed outstandingly above and beyond the call of duty is Sergeant Janice Goldsmith. Her research into the second world war PLUTO programme led to our discovery of the Professor's hiding place in one of the suspect's bungalows.   Janice, would you like to come up here, please?"

Sergeant Goldsmith walked to the front of the room, looking embarrassed as people cheered, clapped and whistled. Willis shook her hand and handed over a scroll with a ribbon tied round it.

Peter Mason took the lead again.

"And I would like to commend Mr George Henley. By his speedy forensics work on Dr Wells' telephone, we were able to eliminate him from the list of suspects and thereby discover the real instigator of the kidnapping."

Cheers went round the room again as George went to the front of the room and received his scroll.

"Thank you, everybody. Please finish the work that you are doing and then write a handover note to DS Dunwoody at the front here. You are then free to leave."

Peter Mason shook Simon Willis's hand and thanked him for his help.

"I hope we keep in touch, Simon."

"Yes that would be nice, either professionally or privately."

"And Detective Sergeant Dunwoody, you've been absolutely wonderful at handling the Professor, as well as my staff."

"Yes, great job, David!" Willis agreed. "Definitely over–performing, as usual."

"Thank you, sirs." Woody looked pleased. "I'm glad the case turned out well in the end."

"Amen to that," Mason agreed.

CHAPTER THIRTY
Farewell Party

LEN was in a deliriously happy frame of mind. Alice had contacted him and said that she wanted to give their marriage another try, and that she had left Dennis because he was a womaniser. Len had played it cool and said they could be 'friends', and see how things went from there. Added to which, all charges against the gang had been quietly dropped and all been released from custody with cautions. He was in his kitchen preparing some lunch when there was a knock at the door. To his surprise, the Professor was standing on his doorstep.

"Mark! Please come in!"

"No, no, I just wanted to say goodbye to you, Len."

"Oh right. Well, that's very good of you, in the circumstances."

The Professor smiled. "Also, I wanted to let you know that the project has been moved to Sandpoint in Dorset. So your railway is safe, for the time being."

"Really? That's fantastic, I'm so relieved. Thank you, Mark!" Len shook his hand.

The Professor smiled. "I told them there were too many holes in the area."

Len roared with laughter. "Too many bad holes, that is?"

"That's right!" Mark laughed back. "So what will you do now? I did ask for leniency but I don't know if that will make any difference."

"We've all been let off! All the charges have been dropped!"

"Well, well," the Professor mused. "I didn't think they would take any notice of me."

"You're obviously more important than you thought!" exclaimed Len. "Good luck with your new invention, I hope it all works out."

"And you too, Len. And remember what I said, you need to get out more."

"Yes, I will. On that note, my wife's been back in touch, she wants us to have another try."

"Excellent news!" The Professor was positively beaming. "I have to say that things have improved somewhat between my ex and I, also."

"Brilliant! Can I shake your hand again?"

The men shook hands vigorously.

"Goodbye, Len. Perhaps we will have that game of golf one day?"

"Goodbye, Mark. Indeed. Well, you know where I am." They both laughed again, then Len watched as the Professor got into his Saab and drove away.

A short while later, Len rang round all the members of the gang and asked them to come round to his house as he had an announcement to make. At six o'clock they were all crammed into Len's shed, busy helping themselves to drinks from his bar. No matter, this was definitely a cause for celebration. Especially now that Derek had returned safe and well, and unbelievably had also been released. Not to mention that George's son, Gary, had been given the million pounds reward, which although he had been instructed not to tell anybody, George had told them anyway.

"Has everybody got a drink?" Len asked.

"Yes!" came multiple replies.

"The reason I've asked you round is I've got an announcement to make. I've heard from the Professor today that the nuclear reprocessing site is being moved to Sandpoint in Dorset."

"Hurray!" came a roar, with glasses and beer cans clinking.

"I wanted to raise a toast to the Professor because, despite everything we put him through, I am positive that he did this as a favour to me – and to the railway, of course – by telling them that the ground was unsuitable, because there were too many holes!"

"Hurray!" came more cheers, as laughter rang round the room.

"And I know that he has put in a good word for us all, which is why we aren't now banged up in high security prisons. Take my word for it, if it wasn't for him sticking up for us, that's where we'd be."

"I'll drink to that!" exclaimed Derek.

"So, here's to the Professor – Mark – may you have good health and happiness, sir, you are a true gentleman."

"The Professor!" they all chanted, before downing their drinks in one.

The End

Thank you for reading my book. A review would
be gratefully received.

Other books by this Author include:

The Silver Cross (Psychic Detective Mysteries #1)
http://www.amazon.co.uk/dp/B00AJMWTVC

The Golden Horn
http://amzn.com/B00HYC2BL8

Blue Angel (London Crime Drama)
www.amazon.co.uk/dp/B0078CPJLS

The Stolen Christmas (Children's Christmas Story)
www.amazon.co.uk/dp/B004NNVBJO

Blog:
junewinton.wordpress.com

twitter:
https://twitter.com/junewinton

Printed in Germany
by Amazon Distribution
GmbH, Leipzig